CONTENTS

PART ONE: Introduction

Study and revision advice

There are two main stages to your reading and work on *Lord of the Flies*. Firstly, the study of the book as you read it. Secondly, your preparation or revision for the exam or controlled assessment. These top tips will help you with both.

READING AND STUDYING THE NOVEL – DEVELOP INDEPENDENCE!

Try to engage and respond **personally** to the characters, ideas and story – not just for your enjoyment, but also because it helps you develop your own, **independent ideas and thoughts** about *Lord of the Flies*. This is something that examiners are very keen to see.

Talk about the text with friends and family; ask questions in class; put forward your own viewpoint – and, if time, **read around** the text to find out about *Lord of the Flies*.

Take time to **consider** and **reflect** about the **key elements** of the novel; keep your own notes, mind-maps, diagrams, scribbled jottings about the characters and how you respond to them; follow the story as it progresses (what do you think might happen?); discuss the main themes and ideas (what do *you* think it is about? Good versus evil?); pick out language that impresses you or makes an **impact**, and so on.

Treat your studying **creatively**. When you write essays or give talks about the novel make your responses creative. Think about using really clear ways of explaining yourself, use unusual **quotations**, well-chosen **vocabulary**, and try powerful, persuasive ways of beginning or ending what you say or write.

REVISION – DEVELOP ROUTINES AND PLANS!

Good revision comes from **good planning**. Find out when your exam or controlled assessment is and then plan to look at key aspects of *Lord of the Flies* on different days or times during your revision period. You could use these Notes – see **How can these Notes help me?** – and add dates or times when you are going to cover a particular topic.

Use **different ways of revising**. Sometimes talking about the text and what you know/don't know with a friend or member of the family can help; other times, filling a sheet of A4 with all your ideas in different colour pens about a character, for example Ralph, can make ideas come alive; other times, making short lists of quotations to learn or numbering events in the plot can assist you.

Practise plans and **essays**. As you get nearer the 'day', start by looking at essay **questions** and writing short bulleted plans. Do several plans (you don't have to write the whole essay); then take those plans and add details to them (quotations, linked ideas). Finally, using the advice in **Part Six: Grade Booster**, write some practice essays and then check them out against the advice we have provided.

EXAMINER'S TIP

Prepare for the exam/controlled assessment! Whatever you need to bring, make sure you have it with you – books, if you're allowed, pens, pencils – and that you turn up on time!

Introducing *Lord of the Flies*

SETTING

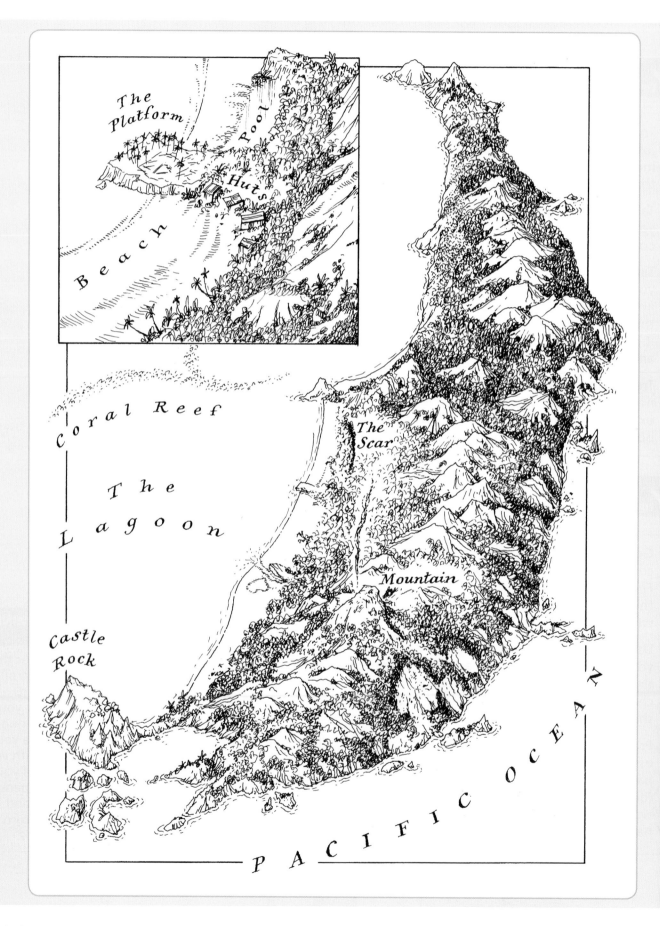

HARACTERS: WHO'S WHO

RALPH
THE ELECTED LEADER.

PIGGY
INTELLIGENT BUT AN
OUTSIDER.

JACK
EX-HEAD BOY.
HUNTER.
ASSUMES
LEADERSHIP.

SIMON
SHY BUT COURAGEOUS.

ROGER
JACK'S CRUEL
LIEUTENANT.

MAURICE
A LOYAL SAVAGE
WITHOUT ROGER'S
BRUTALITY.

SAM AND ERIC
TWINS. OFTEN TREATED AS ONE
PERSON.

THE LITTLUNS
JOHNNY   PERCIVAL

WILLIAM GOLDING: AUTHOR AND CONTEXT

911 William Golding born 19 September in Cornwall

914 Outbreak of the First World War

930 Stock Exchange Crash. Golding joins Brasenose College, Oxford, s an undergraduate

934 Golding works as an actor, producer and writer for a small heatre company

939 Outbreak of the Second World War

940 Golding serves in the Royal Navy in command of a rocket ship, nvolved in the sinking of the *Bismarck*

945 End of the Second World War. Golding teaches at Bishop Wordsworth's School, Salisbury

954 Publication of *Lord of the Flies*

983 Golding awarded the Nobel Prize for Literature

993 Golding dies at his home in Cornwall

PART TWO: PLOT AND ACTION

Plot summary: What happens in *Lord of the Flies*?

REVISION ACTIVITY

- Go through the chapter summaries below and **highlight** what you think is the **key moment** in each section.
- Then find each moment in the **text** and **reread** it. Write down **two reasons** why you think each moment is so **important**.

CHAPTERS ONE AND TWO

- A group of boys are evacuated due to a war involving England. They become marooned on a small island.
- Ralph and Piggy meet and find a conch. Ralph blows the conch to call other survivors, who gather together on the beach.
- A group of choirboys arrive, led by Jack Merridew. They are mostly older boys.
- Ralph is elected leader but Jack is not pleased. Jack and his choir become the hunters.
- Ralph, Jack and Simon explore the island. Jack almost kills a piglet.
- A meeting is called. The conch becomes a symbol of authority.
- The boys argue over the existence of a beast on the island.
- A fire is lit to attract attention but it burns out of control. A boy with a birthmark disappears.

CHAPTERS THREE AND FOUR

- Jack takes delight in tracking pigs but fails to kill any.
- Ralph constructs shelters but with only limited success due to lack of he
- Jack and Ralph argue over priorities.
- Simon goes into the forest alone.
- Roger and Maurice destroy the smaller children's sandcastles. Roger throws stones at Henry.
- Ralph spots a ship. The chance of rescue disappears because the fire is left unattended.
- The hunters return with a pig. Ralph is angry with Jack for letting the fire go out.
- Feeling guilty, Jack lashes out at Piggy and smashes a lens in his glasse
- Ralph is upset and calls a meeting.

CHAPTERS FIVE AND SIX

- Ralph points out the requirements for survival.
- Discussion turns to the 'beastie', which Jack and Piggy dismiss.
- Unseen by the boys, a dead parachutist drifts on to the island near the fire.
- Sam and Eric believe the parachutist to be the beast and rush to tell the others.
- The boys gather on the platform and Jack suggests they hunt the beast.
- Ralph, Jack and the older boys head off together. Piggy stays behind with the 'littluns'.
- Ralph goes alone to the unexplored part of a rocky outcrop where he is soon joined by Jack.

CHAPTERS SEVEN AND EIGHT

Ralph notices how dirty the boys have become.

Ralph and the hunters try to kill a wild boar and, in a frenzy, re-enact the event.

Ralph, Jack and Roger hunt for the beast on the mountain-top. They see the dead parachutist, and think it is the beast.

The boys discuss the beast. Jack believes the hunters can kill it. Ralph knows they are just boys armed with sticks.

Jack unsuccessfully tries to overthrow Ralph as leader. He wanders off, soon secretly joined by many of the older boys.

The hunters kill a sow. They plan to invite the others to a feast with the aim of stealing their fire, and they put the pig's head on a stick.

Simon has a 'conversation' with the pig's head, then falls unconscious.

CHAPTERS NINE AND TEN

- Simon sees the dead parachutist and knows the truth about the beast.
- Ralph and Piggy join the other boys' feast. They dance and chant as thunder strikes.
- Simon stumbles into the tribal circle. He is seen as the beast and killed in a frenzied attack.
- Simon and the parachutist are washed out to sea.
- Ralph, Piggy, Sam and Eric show signs of guilt. Ralph becomes confused.
- Jack and his hunters set up camp on the rocky outcrop.
- Three hunters attack Piggy at night and steal his glasses.

CHAPTERS ELEVEN AND TWELVE

Ralph, Piggy, Sam and Eric decide to confront Jack.

Piggy is killed by a falling rock when Roger leans on a lever, catapulting the rock towards him. The conch is also destroyed.

Sam and Eric are captured by the hunters, leaving Ralph alone.

Jack and his hunters track Ralph as if he is a pig.

Jack sets most of the island on fire in order to flush out Ralph.

As Ralph collapses on the beach, he looks up and sees a naval officer. He is rescued!

Chapter One: The Sound of the Shell

Summary

❶ A group of boys are marooned on an island after evacuation from a war zone.

❷ Ralph and Piggy are first on the scene and use a conch to summon other surviv

❸ The most impressive entrance is made by a group of choirboys led by the red-haired Jack Merridew, head boy and chapter chorister.

❹ One of the choirboys, Simon, faints near the platform where the boys are gathering.

❺ Piggy's nickname is revealed to the boys' general amusement.

❻ The boys elect Ralph as chief. Jack believes the role should be his. He and Ralph agree that the choir will be the hunters, with Jack in charge.

❼ Ralph, Jack and Simon decide to explore the island.

❽ The three boys come across a piglet, which Jack almost kills before hesitating. H declares he will spill blood 'Next time—!' (p. 29).

Why is this chapter important?

A It establishes the **setting** – a desert island.

B Golding introduces us to the **main** characters – Ralph, Piggy, Jack, Simon and Roger – and aspects of their different personalities are revealed.

C After Ralph is elected leader, we learn of his **generosity** when he asks Jack to take charge of the hunters.

D The **importance** of the **conch** is established and it becomes a symbol of authorit

E The **bad weather** on the island foreshadows later events, when Simon is murdered.

The setting – the island

The island setting is described in vivid, physical terms. It is clearly a tropical paradis Notice the words Golding uses to portray its richness and variety – 'reef', 'cirque', 'scar', 'lagoon', 'defiles' (pp. 24–7).

You will see as you read the book that the island is one of many contrasts – high an low, rocky and forested, friendly and unfriendly. It is also 'roughly boat-shaped' (p. 26) – tapering towards one end.

The author does not choose the characters or the setting purely by chance – they all have a deliberate function. The island is exotic but threatening. This is seen immediately when a bird, 'a vision of red and yellow, flashed upwards with a witch like cry' (p. 1).

EXAMINER'S TIP

Read your exam question with care. If it is about the setting and the island, stick to these elements.

GRADE BOOSTER

Think about what is happening in the adult world. Adults are destroying each other in an all-out war, using every weapon available to them. This foreshadows later events, as the savages destroy much of the island.

GRADE BOOSTER

Look at the detail. For example, Jack did not kill the pig because he is not yet far enough removed from civilisation. Later, he does! Another detail is the way in which Piggy is influenced by adults – mostly his aunt.

CHARACTERS – RALPH, PIGGY AND JACK

...ph and Piggy are the first boys we encounter. Ralph is clearly more relaxed on the ...nd, taking the opportunity to go for a swim in the tropical heat. Piggy tries to be ...ndly, confiding to Ralph that 'Piggy' is a nickname.

...gy is fat, suffers from asthma and is far from physically fit. However, he thinks and ...s like an adult and makes intelligent suggestions to Ralph, such as 'We ought to ...e a meeting' (p. 5). Ralph is able to put Piggy's ideas into action.

...k is head chorister and sees himself as a natural leader. When Piggy proposes that ...y make a list of names, Jack ridicules his list. He criticises 'Fatty' (p. 17) for being ... talkative, and thus promotes the idea of physical action and its supremacy over ...ellectual judgement. This foreshadows later events, when Jack shows his intense ...ike for Piggy.

EXAMINER'S TIP: WRITING ABOUT THE BOYS' NAMES

...he names given to the boys are of some significance, if slight. Most of the boys ...ave names that were common and popular before and just after the Second ...World War. Piggy is so named because of his appearance. Have you noticed that ...e never learn his true name?

...nly two names are of biblical origin or are saints' names. These are Simon (the ...postle who carried Christ's cross and was later martyred, i.e. killed for the sake of ...is beliefs) and John (a common form of Jack).

...ck's surname is revealed as Merridew but we do not know many boys' surnames. ...he lack of surnames makes the boys' individuality less obvious.

Chapter Two: Fire on the Mountain

SUMMARY

❶ The three explorers – Ralph, Jack and Simon – return and Ralph blows the conc to call a meeting. He confirms they are on an uninhabited island.

❷ Jack points out that an army is required for hunting, while Ralph is more concerned with immediate practical issues.

❸ The younger boys (the 'littluns') express their concern about a 'beastie' (p. 35) the island.

❹ At Ralph's suggestion, the boys agree to start a fire to attract the attention of passing ships.

❺ Jack offers to keep the fire going – ordering his hunters to work in rotation.

❻ The fire on the mountain-top, started using Piggy's glasses, burns out of contro

❼ Piggy tells the boys they need to 'act proper' (p. 45) if they are to be rescued.

❽ Piggy discovers the boy with the birthmark has disappeared.

WHY IS THIS CHAPTER IMPORTANT?

A It establishes the **idea** that a **beast** might lurk on the island.

B **Ralph** and **Jack's** different **priorities** are shown.

C Golding introduces the idea of lighting a **fire** as a main way of being **rescued**. This will be important throughout the story.

D The idea that the **hunters** watch over the fire will break down later in the nove

E The first **death** occurs, through the boys' carelessness. This death foreshadows later **tragedies**.

JACK AND RALPH: DIFFERENCES

Jack stresses the logical need, as he sees it, for hunters – particularly as they have discovered pigs which could provide them with meat. Jack's cruel streak is hinted at. When he exclaims to the group 'We'll have rules!', he adds 'Then when anyone breaks 'em—' (p. 32), the suggestion being that rule-breakers will be punished.

Ralph, on the other hand, continues to explore more pressing matters. He points out that until the grown-ups come to rescue them, which could take a while, the boys must fend for themselves. He argues that whoever holds the conch can speak telling the boys that the speaker 'won't be interrupted' (p. 31). This will ensure tha discussions remain orderly.

Ralph is positive, mentioning the island is a 'good island' (p. 33). Jack, on the other hand, is negative, wanting punishment for rule-breakers.

KEY QUOTE

Ralph: 'There aren't any grown-ups. We shall have to look after ourselves.' (p. 31)

CHECKPOINT 2

Is the island too small for both Jack and Ralph?

GRADE BOOSTER

Ralph and Jack get on well in this chapter. They grin at each other and share 'that strange invisible light of friendship' (p. 39). Look out for any evidence in the coming chapters that shows the deterioration of their relationship.

THE FIRE AND PIGGY

e fire has two purposes – it is a practical aid to the boys' rescue and a source of . Under normal circumstances boys between six and twelve years of age would be entrusted with fire, even with adult supervision, and certainly not on this le. Notice how the atmosphere changes when the fire becomes not fun but fatal.

gy supports Ralph in this chapter. Ralph has explained their predicament and igests the idea of a fire, but even he does not follow the idea through. It is Piggy o explains the need for smoke not flame. There is **irony** in the fact that although sight is poor ('Jus' blurs, that's all. Hardly see my hand' – p. 40) Piggy's foresight rception and understanding of the consequences of actions) is excellent.

ther, while the boys see the potential for enjoyment of the fire, Piggy sees its sible dangers. His manner and tone in this chapter are almost parental: 'My! u've made a big heap, haven't you?' (p. 40). He also urges the need for practical isiderations, like shelters, after the cold of the previous night.

tice Jack's lack of patience with Piggy. When he needed Piggy's glasses to light the , he 'snatched' (p. 40) them, a verb suggesting rough treatment. Later, the hunters al Piggy's glasses to light their fire. What do the two events tell us about Jack?

EXAMINER'S TIP: WRITING ABOUT THE BEAST

his section is very important because it establishes the fact that there might be mething malevolent and fearsome on the island. The older boys try to dismiss e 'beastie' (p. 34) as a figment of the younger boys' imaginations. One of the lder boys points out that the little boy with the birthmark 'must have had a ightmare' (p. 35).

nce the idea of a 'beastie' is openly spoken about it casts a shadow of doubt all the boys' minds. It signals the end of innocence on the island. Later on in e novel, Piggy rightly mentions that the only evil on the island is the evil in the inds of the boys. Thus, Golding suggests that evil is not external but internal (see ey **contexts: Personal experiences**).

KEY QUOTE

'His voice rose to a shriek of terror as Jack snatched the glasses off his face' (p. 40)

GRADE BOOSTER

Look at the language Golding uses to describe Jack's treatment of Piggy. What does his choice of words tell you?

DID YOU KNOW

Golding was embarrassed about his poems published in 1934. When he found a book of his poems in a second-hand bookshop, he bought it and burned it at home.

KEY QUOTE

Jack: 'If I could only get a pig!' (p. 56)

EXAMINER'S TIP

Evaluate the part played by the hunters in the story so far. Who do they see as leader? Notice how their allegiance to Jack develops as the story progresses.

CHECKPOINT 3

What evidence is there that Jack is fully focused on hunting?

Chapter Three: Huts on the Beach

SUMMARY

❶ Jack goes pig hunting – unsuccessfully.

❷ Ralph shows his sense of responsibility by attempting to build shelters, but these are only partially successful due to lack of help from the rest of the boys, apart from Simon.

❸ Jack develops a fascination for hunting pigs.

❹ Ralph and Jack have a difference of opinion; Jack's obsession with hunting irritates Ralph, who is more concerned with the general well-being of the boys.

❺ Ralph views Jack's hunting as enjoyment.

❻ Simon goes off into the forest on his own.

WHY IS THIS CHAPTER IMPORTANT?

A Golding further develops **Ralph's** character. We see how concerned Ralph is with **practical** matters – mainly keeping a fire burning and constructing shelter

B We learn more about **Simon**.

C With virtually all the boys doing what they want, this foreshadows later events, when the boys willingly turn to **savagery**.

D We witness Jack's growing **fascination** with hunting pigs – that he is willing to spill blood and he enjoys the **thrill of the hunt**.

E We see how some boys act on the **vows** made at the assembly, while others are content to **survive** day by day.

LAW AND ORDER

The boys have come from a society in which orderliness is normal. They attempt to continue this when they first arrive on the island.

Very quickly, the conch has come to symbolise the values of their previous existence. The boys cannot talk at meetings unless they are holding the conch. They are forced to treat whoever is speaking with respect.

This means that Piggy – in many ways a natural victim – is able to air intelligent thoughts that lead to improvements in the boys' lives. These include the suggestion that the toilets are moved away from the shelters and the boys keep a fire going at all times.

'Parliaments' of this kind have always been key elements of successful civilisations. is Jack who challenges this structure. His leadership is more like that of a dictator.

[SI]MON EMERGES AS A CHARACTER

[Si]mon plays a part in this chapter and we learn further information about him. He is [r]epeatedly referred to as being strange in one way or another, but exactly what form [it] takes is never very certain.

[He] is helpful in building the shelters and finding food for the littluns, but he is also [co]ntent to sit alone in the forest. The younger boys follow him about, which seems [to] suggest that he is popular despite being thought of as odd by Ralph.

[Sim]on is difficult to pin down. Although he helps with the shelters, he also likes to [be] alone. At the end of this chapter, Ralph and Jack expect to find Simon in the pool [wi]th the others. However, he has gone into the forest with 'an air of purpose' (p. 57).

[E]XAMINER'S TIP: WRITING ABOUT PIGGY'S GLASSES

[P]iggy's glasses expose the breakdown of law and order. They belong to Piggy, [w]ho needs them to see properly. Used with permission, they start the fires that [a]re seen as essential both for rescue and for hygienically cooked food.

[In] later chapters, Jack refuses to respect Piggy's right to the glasses – first punching [h]im and breaking a lens, then stealing them to light fires. Jack is challenging [R]alph's style of leadership, which has kept things reasonable on the island.

[P]iggy's glasses also represent the idea of possession or ownership – what belongs [t]o whom. By using Piggy's glasses to start the fire, Jack replaces the rule of law [w]ith personal desire and need.

[U]se this information as part of an answer if you are asked to write about law and [o]rder on the island.

? DID YOU KNOW

Golding's novel is partly a reaction to a Victorian book called *Coral Island* (R. M. Ballantyne, 1857) where marooned children get on really well together. Golding thought the story was unrealistic and that groups of children do not behave as the book depicted.

KEY QUOTE

'He was a small, skinny boy, his chin pointed, and his eyes so bright they had deceived Ralph into thinking him delightfully gay and wicked.' (p. 57)

CHECKPOINT 4

What are the hunters doing while Jack is still looking for pigs?

 **GRADE BOOSTER**

Think 'outside the box'. Is a fire essential for rescue or is Ralph as obsessed with keeping the fire going as Jack is with hunting the pigs?

Chapter Four: Painted Faces and Long Hair

SUMMARY

1. The littluns play on the beach but their play is disturbed by Roger and Maurice, who destroy their sandcastles. Roger throws stones close to Henry.

2. Jack paints his face with clay and charcoal and goes hunting.

3. Ralph spies the smoke of a ship on the horizon.

4. He discovers the fire has gone out.

5. The hunters return with a dead pig.

6. Ralph is angry and Piggy backs him up. Jack smashes a lens in Piggy's glasses.

7. Ralph, upset about the fire going out, calls a meeting.

WHY IS THIS CHAPTER IMPORTANT?

A Roger's **cruelty** comes to light.

B With the **successful hunt** – the first occasion where blood is spilt – we are allowed a glimpse into possible **further events**, when human blood is spilt.

C The chance of a **rescue** is **lost** and so the boys are given time to descend into **savagery**.

D In the hunters' chant and re-enactment of the kill we see a **de-civilising proce** emerging.

E Attitudes towards **Piggy** are further exposed, and Golding shows the growing **division** between Jack and Ralph.

ATTITUDES TOWARDS PIGGY

At the bathing pool, Ralph considers Piggy in a negative light, believing him to be ['a bore' (p. 68). At this point in the novel, Ralph thinks Piggy's ideas are 'dull' (p. 68 and he smiles at the prospect of pulling Piggy's leg. However, it is Ralph who, in a later chapter, recognises Piggy's value to the group.

The others see Piggy as 'an outsider' (p. 68). His accent is different, less middle-clas than the other boys'. His size, his asthma and the fact that he wears glasses set him apart. He is of little help in hunting or building shelters, which reinforces the view that he is different and useless.

When Jack breaks his promise by letting the fire go out, he is unable to face up to failure. He realises that the possibility of rescue is far more important than hunting He is confronted by Ralph and also criticised by Piggy, and he lashes out at the easi target – Piggy – breaking a lens in his glasses.

When the boys cook and eat the pig, Piggy asks for meat but Jack points out that is not entitled to any because he did not hunt. Simon, feeling guilty about not hav hunted either, gives his meat to Piggy.

GRADE BOOSTER

Roger emerges as a cruel character during the course of the novel. Here, his cruelty is portrayed for the first time as he destroys the three littluns' sandcastles and kicks sand into Percival's eye. What motive does he have, if any?

CHECKPOINT 5

Who mimics Roger's cruelty?

KEY QUOTE

'The fire was right out, smokeless and dead; the watchers were gone.' (p. 71)

⊣E GROWING GAP BETWEEN RALPH AND JACK

⊣k is determined and single-minded in his pursuit of the pigs yet proud and ⊣gressive in the incident involving Piggy. He apologises for letting the fire go out ⊣t not, significantly, for breaking the glasses.

⊣k lashes out at Piggy partly because he is embarrassed about his mistake, but also ⊣ause he feels cornered. The apology is a painful – and unusual – experience for him.

⊣ph exhibits real despair at the passing of the ship, possibly because he is ⊣ginning to feel the pressure of his overall responsibility for the boys. He has been ⊣olved in work, building the shelters, and the idea that the island is fun is wearing ⊣n. He is also beginning to re-assess the usefulness of his fellow-castaways.

⊣XAMINER'S TIP: WRITING ABOUT THE MOVE AWAY ⊣ROM CIVILISATION

⊣lotice how Jack uses clay as facial camouflage. When the hunters return, they ⊣hant in triumph – having killed a pig. They retell the story of the hunt and ⊣e-enact the kill.

⊣vidence of a gradual de-civilising process is emerging. The boys now display a ⊣ack of cleanliness when eating and their personal hygiene is deteriorating. The ⊣hree-syllable chanting and simplistic replay of the whole event is a move away ⊣rom civilisation.

⊣Vhen you write about this theme be aware of how the move away from ⊣ivilisation becomes more obvious as the novel progresses.

Chapter Five: Beast from Water

SUMMARY

1. Ralph thinks about the seriousness of the forthcoming meeting and of his role chief.

2. At the meeting, he lays down the ground rules for behaviour on the island.

3. Discussion turns to the beast, and some of the boys wonder if they are not alor on the island. Jack and Piggy dismiss the idea.

4. The opinions of Piggy and Simon are ignored.

5. Jack and Ralph have a further disagreement and the meeting ends.

6. Simon and Piggy, fearing what Jack is capable of, urge Ralph to remain as chief

7. Simon, Piggy and Ralph discuss what grown-ups would do, and wish for a signa from them.

WHY IS THIS CHAPTER IMPORTANT?

A Golding's **description** on the first page of this chapter **mirrors** Ralph's **feelings** and we see his increasing unease.

B As Ralph begins to recognise the qualities needed for **leadership**, we notice hi new **respect** for Piggy.

C It is significant that Jack **dismisses** the idea of a **beast** here, for he will later us the boys' fear of it to his own **advantage**.

D Piggy's **logical thinking** and knowledge of **science** lead him to argue that the onl **fear** worth considering is the fear of **people** – an important idea in the novel.

E Simon would like to speak about the **nature of evil** but he is silenced – which foreshadows his death later on, when he tries to bring the truth about the beast to the boys.

RALPH AS LEADER

Ralph is forced to grow up quickly as life takes on a new seriousness for him. He walks on the beach thinking about the boys' initial enthusiasm for the island. He considers how their original ideas for keeping order have broken down and realise that prospects for rescue in the immediate future are not good.

Having decided to call an assembly, he is anxious that it does not turn into a pointle exercise and a wasted opportunity. He thinks beforehand, 'This meeting must not b fun, but business' (p. 81).

Before speaking at the assembly, Ralph considers the weight of his responsibility as chief. He recognises the ability to think rationally and systematically as an importar requirement for leadership. He realises that Piggy is able to think clearly and logica and begins to have a new-found respect for him.

CHECKPOINT 7

What particularly worries Ralph about the boys' adjustment to life on the island?

KEY QUOTE

Piggy: 'I know there isn't no beast – not with claws and all that, I mean – but I know there isn't no fear, either!' (p. 90)

GRADE BOOSTER

Ralph points out that 'the rules are the only thing we've got!' (p. 99). How far have the rules of civilised society broken down so far? It is a useful exercise to track the breakdown of the rules as you go through each chapter.

THE SIGNIFICANCE OF THE BEAST

Although the chapter is called 'Beast from Water', in 'deciding on the fear' (p. 88) a number of explanations are put forward.

The explanations range from real wild creatures, like the giant squid, to humans themselves being the source of fear. Unreal phenomena are also considered – fear created by the imagination, fear of evil and fear of ghosts. Notice how each suggestion is received by the different boys.

The significance of the chapter is that it creates doubt in the minds of the boys that they are alone and introduces the idea of the possibility of something 'other' on the island.

EXAMINER'S TIP: WRITING ABOUT OTHERS' VIEWS ON RALPH

For a top mark, you may need to view one of the boys through the eyes of other characters. Knowing a variety of viewpoints on a particular person is important as together they give a balanced insight into a character's personality.

Jack has a lack of respect for the authority of the conch as well as a lack of respect for Ralph as leader. This leads Jack to break the rules. When confronted by Ralph, he shouts and swears. His use of bad language appears to demonstrate his contempt for any sort of authority.

Piggy, on the other hand, fears for his own position if Ralph were no longer leader. He is afraid of what Jack might do if Jack became leader.

Simon is clear and straightforward in his statement that Ralph should remain as leader: 'Go on being chief' (p. 101).

CHECKPOINT 8

Why might Piggy be fearful of people?

GRADE BOOSTER

To aim for a top grade, you will need to know how the characters shape and react to events. For example, notice how Jack and Piggy treat the younger boys, when the fear of the beast is mentioned. Who is the kinder of the two?

When commenting on Golding's use of description, point out that his natural descriptions are mingled with events. The first two paragraphs of this chapter set the scene and action. Golding writes 'A sliver of moon rose over the horizon' (p. 103), going on to describe the battle from the vantage point of the island. Notice 'but there were other lights in the sky, that moved fast, winked, or went out' (p. 103).

KEY QUOTE

Sam and Eric: 'It kind of sat up—' (p. 109)

CHECKPOINT 9

What is the significance of the parachutist?

Chapter Six: Beast from Air

SUMMARY

1. A dead parachutist lands on the island.
2. As Sam and Eric tend the fire, they mistake the parachutist for the beast.
3. At a meeting, Jack announces that the beast should be hunted down and he ridicules the importance of the conch.
4. The bigger boys, without Piggy, set off to find the beast.
5. Ralph bravely goes first to the unexplored part of a rocky outcrop. He is soon joined by Jack.
6. The boys discover that the end of the island would be a good place for a fort.
7. Ralph stresses the boys' practical needs and the others reluctantly go on with the journey.

WHY IS THIS CHAPTER IMPORTANT?

A The **dead parachutist** is seen as the **beast**, which has huge implications for the group.

B The role of **Sam** and **Eric**, speaking as **one voice**, is evident in this chapter. Their description of the beast is terrifying – more so because of the two boys' simultaneous account.

C The revelation that the **beast** exists is reassuring as it is now **recognised** as real, something that can be hunted. This reinforces the **importance** of Jack's hunters.

D The **conch** loses importance as the need to hunt down the beast now dominates the boys' minds. Golding shows us **Ralph**'s **leadership qualities** and **bravery** in action.

E The **differences** between Jack and Piggy are further highlighted.

F Simon begins to **understand** the **true nature** of the beast.

SIGHTING THE BEAST

The boys wanted a sign from the grown-ups. They do not get what they expected! Ten miles above them a battle is being fought and a 'sign' comes down in the form of a parachutist.

The world of grown-ups is a fearful place, involved as it is in a war involving the atomic bomb. The grown-ups are doing no better than their male offspring. Sending a 'beast' as a sign is, therefore, appropriate.

He lands on the mountain where the breeze and the parachute's suspension lines control his body like the strings of a puppet. In the early morning darkness, Eric hears the sound of the parachute canopy. Neither he nor Sam can see very clearly and, believing they have seen the 'beast', they run away in terror.

Ralph's willingness to call an assembly shows that he is aware of the near panic of the previous evening. The twins' description of the thing they saw terrifies the other boys. Jack, though, suddenly has new power. There is no longer a debate that the hunters are needed: they are now defenders!

KEY QUOTE

'However Simon thought of the beast, there rose before his inward sight the picture of a human at once heroic and sick.' (p. 112)

EXAMINER'S TIP

Simon emerges as a complex and important minor character. Despite the fact that he says and does comparatively little, his speech and actions are highly significant. Take careful note of what happens whenever his name is mentioned.

⅃CK AND PIGGY – VERY DIFFERENT PEOPLE

k is delighted at the prospect of a hunt. At last, the power is shifting his way. He is e to ridicule Piggy's fear of the beast and the importance of the conch, seeing the al of holding the conch to speak to the assembly as pointless and unproductive.

s Jack who initially leads Ralph and the bigger boys in search of the beast. They k around the tail end of the island – the only part Jack previously failed to visit. k is aggressive, physically able and impulsive.

gy is not physically active. However, he is intelligent and able to express his ideas d opinions. Despite dismissing ghosts earlier, he admits to being frightened, ggesting that they stay where they are rather than search for the beast.

EXAMINER'S TIP: WRITING ABOUT COURAGE

alph's courage is shown throughout this chapter. He displays common sense and n almost obsessive determination.

e attempts, despite Jack's resentment, to push through some of the points he nade during the previous night's assembly. He bravely leads the exploration of he far end of the island, and shows moral courage in facing up to Jack over the upremacy of the conch.

despite Jack's bravado and Piggy's thinking skills, neither of them shows the ourage of his convictions. Jack is keen to hunt the beast but finally cannot do so. While Piggy's rational mind may tell him ghosts do not exist, he declares his fear f the beast and stays to look after the littluns.

DID YOU KNOW

Golding was keen on books on psychology.

Chapter Seven: Shadows and Tall Trees

SUMMARY

❶ Ralph is dismayed by the dirty state of the boys and considers the harsher terrai[n] of the other side of the island.

❷ Simon tries to reassure Ralph that he'll get home safely.

❸ Jack discovers the tracks of a wild boar.

❹ The boys make up a ritual dance to celebrate the hunt. They claim it is just a game, but Robert is hurt.

❺ Ralph, Jack and Roger hunt for the beast on the mountain-top. They discover th[e] dead parachutist whom they assume is the beast.

❻ Terrified by their discovery, they flee down the mountain.

WHY IS THIS CHAPTER IMPORTANT?

A We see further evidence of the boys' **decline** through **Ralph's observations** about their lack of cleanliness.

B We witness Ralph's awe at the immensity and power of the **ocean**, which he sees as a **barrier** between the island and the civilised world.

C Ralph's **reflections** on the **comforts** of his typically English middle-class home provide a contrast between the **civilised adult world** and the **island**. There is a sense of **loss**.

D The boys' playful **re-enactment** of their hunt is yet further evidence of the boys' descent into **savagery**.

E Golding develops the theme of **leadership**, as Jack and Ralph try to prove their **courage** and right to lead.

NATURAL IMAGES

Natural images and descriptions are plentiful in this chapter. Ralph's continuing thoughts about the vastness of the sea (see Chapter Six) are repeated at greater leng[th]

The description of the forest is vivid; the undergrowth on one side is impassable, th[e] sea and the cliffs on the other are threatening. This gives emphasis to the fact that the boys are trapped on the island.

Ralph called the island 'good' (Chapter Two, p. 33) but in this chapter the natural forces appear hostile. Ralph is able to understand the power of the sea against humanity. The sea has the power to 'suck down' (p. 120). Golding uses a simile, comparing the seaweed to 'shining hair' (p. 121) – which reinforces the sea's streng[th]

The author uses description of the natural elements to show the reader 'the divider the barrier' (p. 121) between the world of adults and the boys' world.

CHECKPOINT 10

What is the value of Simon's imagination?

KEY QUOTE

Jack: 'we need meat even if we are hunting the other thing.' (p. 122)

CHECKPOINT 11

What is the source of the rising tension between Jack and Ralph?

RIBAL DANCE

e enactment of the hunt is reminiscent of tribal dances, which are a ritualistic
resentation of a successful hunt that the tribe hopes for in the future. This,
pled with Jack's mask and the rallying chant of earlier chapters, highlights the
ve away from conventional behaviour. It also shows us the descent into paganism,
beliefs outside of the main world religions.

first, the enactment is controlled, the boys were 'all jabbing at Robert who made
ck rushes' (p. 125). Soon, 'Robert was screaming and struggling with the strength
frenzy' (p. 125), and is eventually reduced to 'frightened snivels' (p. 125).

tice how the enactment almost gets out of control. Ralph is 'carried away' by the
ment. This shows that the desire to hunt and kill is deep within the male human
che. This makes Simon's murder believable in a later chapter.

e sentences in this part of the chapter are short and they are interspersed with
ort speeches, which are either pleas or commands.

XAMINER'S TIP: WRITING ABOUT THE USE OF ANGUAGE

olding uses a flashback – Ralph pondering on his previous existence in
evonport – to create a further contrast between life on the island and the boys'
revious lives.

olding also uses carefully chosen words such as 'uncompromising', 'impossible'
nd 'sheer' (p. 128) to suggest the boys' isolation. This word choice now gives the
npression that the island is a prison rather than a *Coral Island*-type paradise.

s you read through this chapter, notice how Golding further implies the idea
hat the island is a hostile place.

emember to mention the linguistic devices and figurative language used – such
s similes and metaphors.

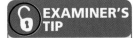

KEY QUOTE

'Kill him! Kill
him!' (p. 125)

EXAMINER'S TIP

Notice how some
of the themes
are developed
in this chapter.
They include
crowd mentality,
civilisation versus
tribalism and the
qualities needed
for leadership.

Chapter Eight: Gift for the Darkness

Summary

① Ralph, Jack and Roger report what they have seen. Jack argues that the hunters can kill the beast.

② Ralph describes the hunters as 'Boys armed with sticks' (p. 137), which hurts Jac

③ Jack tries to overthrow Ralph as leader but he is rejected as the new chief and leaves, soon to be joined by most of the older boys.

④ A fire is relit by the platform.

⑤ Jack goes off with his hunters to kill pigs. They kill a sow who has piglets and decide to invite the others to a feast in order to steal their fire.

⑥ They sever the sow's head and put it on a stick.

⑦ Simon, alone in the forest, sees the pig's head and has a 'conversation' with it, before losing consciousness.

CHECKPOINT 12

What are Piggy's feelings when Jack departs?

Why is this chapter important?

A It shows just how much Jack **hates** Ralph.

B Golding highlights Ralph and Piggy's **realistic approach** when they concede that the boys would be **powerless** against a beast.

C The chapter signals the **split** of the **survivors** into two groups: the **conch group** and the **hunters**. This is the natural development of the differences between the two main **characters**.

D There is further evidence that Jack's style of leadership is a descent into the **primitive**. Debate and discussion are replaced by rehearsed and ritualised responses: 'The Chief has spoken' (p. 155).

E We witness Simon's strange behaviour when he communicates with the 'Lord of the Flies' (p. 157), but we also see a **courageous** side to his character.

KEY QUOTE

Ralph: 'what makes things break up like they do?' (p. 154)

CHECKPOINT 13

What does the voice of the school master represent?

Jack as a leader

Jack is upset by Ralph's analysis of the boys' abilities. Piggy senses that there will be trouble and he tells Ralph, 'Now you done it. You been rude about his hunters' (p. 13

It is Jack who, for the first time, blows the conch and calls an assembly. Here he conforms to law and order and hopes to use it to his advantage. The first words he utters relate to the beast. When questioned, he shouts, 'Quiet!' and 'You listen' (p. 138), signs that debate will not be permitted.

Jack informs his hunters that he's 'going to be chief' (p. 146) and he becomes an authoritarian leader, making it clear that those who disobey will be punished. Whe the hunters find a sow with her piglets the **atmosphere** is both tense and violent.

Jack attempts to persuade the others that there is no beast. It appears that he hedges his bets or deliberately uses the fear of a beast to his own advantage. This why he offers the pig's head as a gift. The possible existence of a beast gives a new importance to Jack's hunters. They are now defending the boys.

⌐E LORD OF THE FLIES

⌐ere are references in ancient history to a 'god of the flies' being worshipped by ⌐gan civilisations. Although Jack has said that they are going to forget about the ⌐ast, the pig's head is still left as a gift. This can be seen as **symbolic** as primitive ⌐n left offerings to pagan gods. Jack's tribe has descended into paganism.

⌐ere is a grudging acceptance of, and respect for, this unnamed being that has been ⌐sed to the status of a god. There is a parallel between the way the boys refer to ⌐eir 'god' – the Lord of the Flies – and the way that they idolise Jack. Jack is, in a ⌐nse, lord over them – his own flies, or menials.

⌐mon's behaviour raises certain questions. We already know he is prone to fainting; ⌐ Chapter Nine it appears he is epileptic: 'Simon's fit passed' (p. 160). His actions, ⌐en, may be governed by his medical condition and he may be hallucinating. ⌐wever, he seems to understand and sympathise with the creature in an almost ⌐ ritual sense.

⌐XAMINER'S TIP: WRITING ABOUT RALPH AND ⌐IGGY'S FEELINGS

⌐he split into two groups was anticipated in earlier chapters. Ralph is initially ⌐ewildered by Jack's departure and feels he will come back. Piggy, however, is ⌐elieved by Jack's departure.

⌐iggy and Ralph consider reorganising things and making a list of names – only to ⌐ind that many of the older boys have drifted away. They suspect that these, like ⌐ack, are the trouble-makers.

⌐alph believes they are better off without Jack. Neither Ralph nor Piggy can ⌐oresee that Jack and his hunters will not leave their group alone ... until they are ⌐estroyed.

Chapter Nine: A View to a Death

SUMMARY

1. Simon sees the dead parachutist and discovers the truth about the beast. He heads off to tell the others.

2. Ralph and Piggy join Jack's party where they are eating meat and having a feast.

3. Jack asks who will join his tribe and he and Ralph argue over where the conch can be used.

4. There is a thunderstorm and Piggy senses trouble.

5. Jack encourages his tribe to do their dance.

6. Simon stumbles into the dancing circle.

7. The boys see Simon as the beast and kill him in a frenzied attack.

8. The bodies of Simon and the parachutist are washed out to sea.

WHY IS THIS CHAPTER IMPORTANT?

A It shows the **contrast** between both Jack's camp and the earlier assemblies, and Jack and Ralph's leadership styles.

B Simon discovers the **truth** concerning the beast but is unable to bring the truth to the others.

C Simon's death marks a **change** in the hunters' **attitude** towards **death**. It also allows Jack to play on the boys' fears.

D The death also brings about a **burden of guilt** as all took part in the murder.

E Golding uses **nature**, **colour** and imagery to effect in the chapter.

F The **disappearance** of the **parachutist's body** is a convenient **plot device**, as it removes the possibility that it will be discovered and revealed for what it is.

FORESHADOWING THE DRAMATIC EVENTS

The heat is oppressive as the thunder clouds gather. Golding has introduced natural forces in this chapter, to re-introduce later when the chanting and dancing is at its height. This makes Simon's murder dramatic and plausible.

Piggy has a headache, which makes him yearn for cool rain. Piggy and Ralph decide to visit Jack's camp to have some meat. Piggy again shows himself to be both parental and protective in his anxiety to visit Jack's camp 'to make sure nothing happens' (p. 163).

What do you think Piggy feared might occur? Could even Piggy have anticipated the outcome of the dance? Is it significant that, like Simon, Piggy has a headache just before the dramatic events happen?

MON – THE MARTYR FOR THE TRUTH

...on is determined to reach the top of the mountain where, in a sense, the truth – both literally and metaphorically. Simon frees the dead airman, who is then given ...dignity of a burial at sea. Simon, too, is consigned to the sea after his murder.

...e news of 'a body on the hill' (p. 169) provides a clear piece of Christian imagery. ...on can be viewed as a prophet and visionary, with a parallel between the ...achutist on the mountain and Christ on the hill at Calvary. The description of ... halo of creatures that surround him with light as he floats out to sea is both ...gnant and significant.

...e fact that Simon's news is ignored by the boys may also be worth some ...sideration – is Golding saying that Christ's message to us is, on the whole, ignored?

XAMINER'S TIP: WRITING ABOUT NATURE AND ...OLOUR

...ature and colour are used to great effect in this chapter. Golding's description ...f the bad weather coming onto the island actually opens the chapter and is ...etailed. He mentions that colours 'drained from water and trees' (p. 160) and ...ontrasts this with the 'spilt guts' (p. 160) of the pig, that 'look like a heap of ...listening coal' (p. 160). The blood that 'gushed out' (p. 160) from Simon's nose ...ould be red and this adds another contrast to colourless nature, as the storm ...aches the island.

...urther into the chapter, Ralph notices the flames against the 'dull light' (p. 165). ...e is able to recognise the beginning of a storm. When evening arrives, he sees ...is come 'not with calm beauty but with the threat of violence' (p. 165). This ...dicates that nature is in harmony with the events that are about to unfold.

...hen lightning strikes, it is described as a 'blue-white scar' (p. 168). During the ...imax of chanting, dancing, thunder and lightning, Simon emerges from the ...ndergrowth. Finally, stars in the night sky pick out strange, luminous creatures ...hich surround Simon's body with light.

...olding has cleverly used neutral nature as a hostile force to make the boys ...fraid. When they see Simon, it is through flashes of lightning and in the dark ...lmost like a strobe-light effect). This makes it believable that they see Simon as ...e beast.

CHECKPOINT 16

What fate do Simon and the parachutist share?

DID YOU KNOW

Golding was a Christian.

KEY QUOTE

Notice how the narrative perspective shifts so that we see Simon as 'the beast' through the boys' eyes: 'The beast was on its knees in the centre, its arms folded over its face.' (p. 168)

Chapter Ten: The Shell and the Glasses

SUMMARY

❶ Piggy and Ralph talk about the events of the previous night.

❷ Sam and Eric join them. Guilt-ridden, the four boys lie to each other about their involvement.

❸ Jack and his hunters set up camp at the far end of the island.

❹ Ralph, Piggy and the twins try, unsuccessfully, to re-light the fire. Ralph shows signs of confusion and they give up on the fire for the evening.

❺ In their shelters that night, they hear noises outside.

❻ Jack and two of his hunters attack and steal Piggy's glasses.

❼ Jack is delighted at his achievement – 'He was a chief now in truth' (p. 186).

WHY IS THIS CHAPTER IMPORTANT?

A We witness **discussions** about Simon's death, which Piggy insists was an **accident**.

B Now that Jack has become **chief** we understand that he has **unchecked power**.

C When one of the boys, Wilfred, is punished for some undisclosed offence, this demonstrates Jack's **authoritarian** leadership.

D Golding shows how Jack is revered and set apart as important in his camp, where he is chief. This **contrasts** sharply with the assemblies, where everyone was considered of **equal value**.

E We learn how the hunters, under Jack's leadership, are willing to use **violence** to obtain what they want – in this case, Piggy's glasses.

THE AFTERMATH OF SIMON'S MURDER

The tone of this chapter is one of hopelessness and gloom among both the conch group and the savages of Castle Rock following Simon's murder. Interestingly, both groups, in one way or another, try to brush the incident aside by childish denials.

Is it too far-fetched to suggest that the three-fold denial by the boys is an allegory for the biblical account of Simon Peter, who denied his knowledge of Christ on three occasions 'before the cock crowed'? This aside, it is only Ralph who recognises the death for what it is – murder.

It is useful to reflect on what all the boys have experienced during their time on the island – fear, deprivation, discomfort, lack of parental care, illness, intimidation and depression. After all this comes the terrible crime of murder – a crime of which they are all guilty in a sense.

CHECKPOINT 17

How does Piggy avoid his feelings of guilt for the death of Simon?

EXAMINER'S TIP

Ralph and Eric, by accident, fight each other in the darkness. Could this symbolise the pointlessness of violence – used without thought or reason?

DID YOU KNOW

The day when *Lord of the Flies* was published a zinc bath packed with ice and bottles of champagne appeared in the staff room at Golding's school.

E SHELL AND THE GLASSES AS SYMBOLS

chapter is entitled 'The Shell and the Glasses', both of which are symbols. The
could represent democracy, the voice of reason or decency. It is of no use in
beyond being a beautiful object – its use is in what it represents or symbolises
he boys.

glasses are useful to Piggy, but have a function beyond that for everyone else
ey can start a fire. The ability to make fire is something that sets human beings
rt from animals. The glasses, therefore, symbolise fire, but also knowledge –
ghtenment – and mastery over primitive instincts.

notable that Piggy perceives the conch as the more valuable item; holding it –
ally – with respect and affection during the events of the next chapter.

XAMINER's tip: Writing about Jack as leader

is chapter shows Jack's camp, now set up at Castle Rock. It is guarded by
ntries who challenge Roger. He says he could still climb up the rock if he wanted
, at which they show him a simple device to deter unwelcome visitors.

e device is a lever pushed under the highest rock, so that it can be dropped on
emies approaching along the narrow strip of land leading to the camp. Jack
viously planned this device to do harm – to Ralph and friends or to the beast?

ger (the cruellest hunter) admires the ingenuity of Jack, whom he regards as a
oper Chief' (p. 176). It is Jack who orders the attack on Ralph's group to steal
ggy's glasses. The organisation of Jack's group is significant. He is placed in a
ominent position with a semi-circle of boys around him, and is almost revered as
jod.

ck denies that the boys killed Simon and warns them about the beast, saying
ey 'can't tell what he might do' (p. 178). He suggests they leave the head of
ch kill as a gift to keep favour with it.

olding lived through the era of dictators in the 1930s and 40s. Is Jack pagan in
s outlook or has he established a dictatorship? His style and the way he assumes
adership could be compared to Hitler, Mussolini and Stalin.

KEY QUOTE

Jack: 'He came
— disguised. He
may come again
even though we
gave him the
head of our kill
to eat.' (p. 177)

CHECKPOINT 18

How does Jack
conduct his
meetings?

GRADE BOOSTER

Thinking
originally, does
Jack believe in
the beast or is
he using fear
as a method of
control?

Chapter Eleven: Castle Rock

SUMMARY

❶ Ralph is unable to light the fire without Piggy's glasses.

❷ The conch group decide to confront Jack and his hunters.

❸ A scuffle breaks out between the two groups at Castle Rock.

❹ Roger leans on the lever which catapults a heavy rock towards Piggy.

❺ Piggy is killed by the falling rock and the conch is destroyed.

❻ Sam and Eric are captured by the hunters.

❼ Ralph is now alone, forced to escape as hunters hurl spears in his direction.

WHY IS THIS CHAPTER IMPORTANT?

A Despite Jack's **crimes**, we see that Ralph intends to approach him as a **civilised human being** and explain the seriousness of the situation.

B Piggy's faith in the ultimate **power** of the **conch** is exhibited when he proudly carries the shell to Castle Rock.

C It is evident that **Sam** and **Eric** are forced to join **Jack's savages** through **violent coercion** rather than **reason**; the rule of law is coming to an end.

D When the conch is shattered and Piggy is killed, both the symbol of **civilised behaviour** and the **voice of reason** are destroyed.

E With the rest of his group gone, Golding shows us how Ralph copes with being the **sole target** of the others' hatred.

THE DEATH OF PIGGY

There is a clear parallel between the death of the pigs and the death of Piggy. Look at Piggy's demise – 'arms and legs twitched a bit, like a pig's after it has been killed' (p. 201) – and note the similarities between that and the graphic, earlier accounts of pig killings (in Chapter Eight, for example).

The focus on Piggy as 'the centre of social derision' (Chapter Nine, p. 165) – a source of amusement – ends. Previously, the humour had been caused by slapstick (falling off the 'twister' log – Chapter Five, p. 82 – at the assembly):

● pantomime mimicry (Maurice pretending to be the pig – Chapter Four, p. 79)

● the Billy Bunter-like earnestness of Piggy ('the tribe were curious to hear what amusing thing he might have to say' – Chapter Eleven, p. 199; see **Key contexts: Boys' behaviour**).

Schoolboy humour, or indeed fun of any sort, is not seen after Piggy's death.

CHECKPOINT 19

What, says Piggy, is the one thing Jack hasn't got?

KEY QUOTE

Piggy: 'You're Chief, Ralph. You remember everything.' (p. 192)

? DID YOU KNOW

'Billy Bunter' was a series of books about a fictitious public schoolboy. He was considered to be a joke figure who liked his food. The first Bunter story (which evolved from earlier comic stories) was published in 1947 by Frank Richards. The stories were so popular a TV series emerged in the 1950s, which was about Billy Bunter's exploits at Greyfriars School. Reading *Lord of the Flies* in the 1960s, people would have identified Piggy as a Billy Bunter type.

KEY QUOTE

Ralph: 'Which is better – to have rules and agree, or to hunt and kill?'(p. 200)

┘ INCREASE IN VIOLENCE

erstandably in a novel featuring schoolboys, play is a prominent form of
aviour and is in evidence when the boys are first on the island. Play in nature is
n practice for something else – play fighting prepares animals for hunting, for
mple. In human beings it may develop beyond the need for survival into more
histicated social skills.

er's stone throwing became dangerous and Jack's exaggerated dominance in the
ne' becomes sinister. When Piggy is killed and the conch destroyed, Jack has no
orse, declaring boldly to Ralph, 'There isn't a tribe for you any more!'(p. 201). He
s, significantly, 'The conch is gone—' (p. 201). The old rules are over; childhood
ocence is lost!

en Jack hurls his spear at Ralph, 'Viciously, with full intention' (p. 201), this is no
ne. He clearly means to wound Ralph, who represents the opposition.

XAMINER'S TIP: WRITING ABOUT THE RULE OF LAW

Castle Rock, Piggy, like Ralph, feels passionately that Jack should respond out
common decency and respect for the rule of law. When Ralph blows the conch,
believes the boys will respond to his call for an assembly.

hen Ralph confronts Jack about the theft, Jack retaliates and a scuffle breaks
t. It is Piggy who reminds Ralph what they came for.

:k has not responded well to the sound of the conch. In fact, he orders his
/ages to capture Sam and Eric, who protest 'out of the heart of civilization'
198). After Piggy's death, and the destruction of the conch, there is no rule
law.

GLOSSARY

social derision ridicule or mockery by society

Chapter Twelve: Cry of the Hunters

SUMMARY

❶ Ralph considers his options as he tries to hide and avoid danger.

❷ He encounters the pig's head and experiences fear and anger, lashing out at it and taking away the spear that supported it.

❸ Ralph goes to speak to Sam and Eric at Castle Rock, but their manner is discouraging, telling Ralph that Roger has 'sharpened a stick at both ends' (p. 2

❹ Ralph becomes aware that he is totally alone.

❺ Jack and the hunters track Ralph as if he were an animal.

❻ Jack sets most of the island on fire to smoke Ralph out.

❼ The smoke from the fire is seen by a passing ship.

❽ Ralph, exhausted, collapses on the beach. He looks up to see the friendly face rescuing naval officer.

KEY QUOTE

Sam and Eric: 'They're going to hunt you to-morrow.' (p. 209)

CHECKPOINT 20

What might the pig's head represent for Ralph?

KEY QUOTE

Naval officer: 'What have you been doing? Having a war or something?' (p. 223)

WHY IS THIS CHAPTER IMPORTANT?

A As Ralph **spies** on Castle Rock, we appreciate how hard it is for him to come t terms with **all that has happened**.

B When Ralph sees the remains of the **pig's head** we are reminded of **Simon's** earlier, very different reaction to the object.

C Ralph fails to see the significance of the sharpened stick, but we realise that I will be **hunted** like a pig.

D When rescuing the boys, the naval officer sees Jack as a **little boy**, rather than seeing his primitive, underlying aggression and savagery.

E Golding makes it clear that it is only **external intervention** that saves Ralph from certain death.

ROGER AND THE SAVAGES

Roger has become sadistic, Sam and Eric calling him 'a terror' (p. 210). He is prepa to kill and behead Ralph, placing Ralph's head on the stick instead of a pig's head This is why the stick is sharpened 'at both ends' (p. 211).

The hunters are now clearly savages. The savages will sweep across the island in li to catch Ralph – communicating (like primitive man) with wavering cries. They lev one of the rocks on the cliff top and it crashes into the thicket, missing him. The savages cheer as it falls – having lost all their humanity.

Under Jack's direction, the savages set the forest on fire with the aim of smoking Ralph out. The raging fire burns the fruit trees – a valuable food source.

ESCUE AT LAST

...ph, the only boy left who has some vestiges of civilised behaviour, can hear the ...al dancing and see savages keeping lookout.

... regrets his isolation and discovers that Jack intends to hunt him like a pig. As he ...ds towards the forest, the cries of the hunters sweep the island behind him.

... ironic that the smoke and fire made to flush out Ralph is their means of rescue. ...sumably, if rescue had not come, Ralph would have been murdered and the island ...uld have been destroyed by fire.

EXAMINER'S TIP: WRITING ABOUT NATURE – FURTHER HOUGHTS

...otice how Ralph is 'scratched and bruised from his flight through the forest' ...o. 203). He is unable to bathe his wounds, as he does not feel safe from Jack's ...ibe 'by the little stream or on the open beach' (p. 203).

...he hunters 'had rushed back to the sunny rock as if terrified of the darkness ...nder the leaves' (p. 203). The hunters are, presumably, afraid of encountering ...alph rather than afraid of the darkness. At this point in the novel, nature comes ...o Ralph's aid as he 'sneaked forward to the edge of that impenetrable thicket' ...pp. 203–4).

...lotice how, in the final chapter, light and dark are used to describe the trees and ...oliage. This could represent the good and bad in us all.

EXAMINER'S TIP

As readers, we are given 'insight' into events that the characters do not always have. This is called dramatic irony. How can you tell that Ralph does not appreciate the danger he is in?

DID YOU KNOW

Twenty-one publishers rejected *Lord of the Flies* before Faber and Faber published it.

Progress and revision check

REVISION ACTIVITY

❶ How does Ralph call other survivors on the island? (Write your answers below)

....

❷ What happens when Ralph spots a ship on the horizon?

....

❸ How does Jack light the first fire?

....

❹ Why does Jack try to overthrow Ralph as leader?

....

❺ Why do Ralph, Piggy, Sam and Eric decide to confront Jack?

....

REVISION ACTIVITY

On a piece of paper write down answers to these questions:

● What are the early indications to suggest the boys will end up fighting each other?

Start: *We know that there is a war in the adult world because ...*

● Is the island good or bad?

Start: *Although Ralph calls the island good, the bad weather on the island symbolises ...*

GRADE BOOSTER

Answer this longer, practice question about the plot/action of the novel:

Q: In what ways could it be said that the novel is a complex one? Think about ...

● The way the de-civilising process takes place

● The way in which the description of the island and the weather often foreshadow future events

● The fact that some of the boys alter their opinions about things and people as the novel progresses

For a C grade: convey your ideas clearly and appropriately (you could use the words from the question to guide your answer) and refer to details from the text (use specific examples).

For an A grade: make sure you comment on the varied ways the story is structured and, if possible, come up with your own or alternative ideas.

Ralph

WHO IS RALPH?

...ph is the chief. He uses the conch to control meetings. He ...the responsibility of looking after the other survivors.

WHAT DOES RALPH DO IN THE NOVEL?

Ralph uses the conch to summon other survivors (see pp. 11–12).

Ralph builds a fire to help the boys get rescued (see p. 37).

Ralph attempts to build shelters for the younger boys (see p. 50).

Ralph raises issues to aid survival and rescue (see pp. 84–8).

Ralph shows courage, exploring a part of the island where the other boys think the beast may lurk (see pp. 114–15).

Ralph is hunted by the savages and is saved by the naval officer (see p. 222).

HOW IS RALPH DESCRIBED AND WHAT DOES IT MEAN?

Quotation	Means?
...here was a mildness about his ...outh and eyes that proclaimed ...o devil.'	The description suggests that he has no hidden depths or unhealthy character traits.
...hey'll see our smoke.'	Ralph believes that rescue from the island is essential. His efforts are directed to keeping the fire going. He is annoyed when Jack and the hunters allow it to go out.
...ew understanding that Piggy ...ad given him.'	Ralph's ability to think things through is attributed to Piggy, whose qualities Ralph begins to admire. Ralph listens to Piggy's advice.
...on't you understand, Piggy? ...he things we did—'	Only Ralph is able to come to terms with the reasons why Simon was killed. He is willing to share the blame and responsibility for Simon's death. This shows his true leadership qualities.

GRADE BOOSTER

To boost your own ideas, find two more quotations about Ralph. Draw your own table and write in the second column what you think each quotation means.

GRADE BOOSTER

Try making a list of Ralph's qualities. For example: (1) Ralph is able to see the good in people and in the island; (2) he is easy to like and naturally at ease; (3) he is tall, blond, good-looking and one of the older boys; (4) he is able to speak at meeting and he considers other people; (5) he is a natural leader.

EXAMINER'S TIP: WRITING ABOUT RALPH

...When you are writing about Ralph, remember that although he is cruel and ...ismissive of Piggy at the start of the novel, he does not possess Jack's malice. ...aving upset Piggy by using his nickname to raise a laugh, he appreciates Piggy's ...ense of humiliation and finds a way out: 'Better Piggy than Fatty ... I'm sorry if ...ou feel like that' (Chapter One, pp. 21–22). Ralph's views change towards Piggy ...s the novel progresses. Through Piggy, Ralph learns to take his responsibilities ...eriously – thinking of rescue and shelter.

Jack

WHO IS JACK?

Jack is leader of the choirboys, who become his hunters. He is a rival to Ralph and eventually declares himself as chief.

WHAT DOES JACK DO IN THE NOVEL?

- Jack decides the choir will be hunters (see p. 19).
- Jack snatches Piggy's glasses to make a fire (see p. 40).
- Jack kills a pig and organises a chant and dance to celebrate the pig's death (see p. 72).
- Jack has disregard for rules (see p. 99).
- When Ralph is re-elected as chief, Jack runs off (see pp. 139–140).
- Jack becomes a cruel leader of his tribe (see p. 201).

HOW IS JACK DESCRIBED AND WHAT DOES IT MEAN?

Quotation	Means?
'This was the voice of one who knew his own mind.'	This suggests that Jack is someone who does not want to obey.
Jack had a 'compulsion to track down and kill that was swallowing him up.'	Although Jack provides the boys with meat, he has an almost addictive urge to kill. He represents Man the Hunter and exhibits a basic, primeval instinct to hunt.
'Do our dance! Come on! Dance!'	Jack turns from hunting pigs to hunting people. He is the one who sets in motion the sequence of events that lead to Simon's death
'the mask was a thing on its own, behind which Jack hid, liberated from shame and self-consciousness'	When painted, Jack feels he can act as he wishes. The mask makes him act in an extreme or evil way.

EXAMINER'S TIP: WRITING ABOUT JACK

Golding has clearly intended you to dislike Jack. His dramatic entrance – the procession of capped and gowned choirboys – is both sinister and anachronistic (out of date) in our time and when the novel was published. He is portrayed as arrogant and aggravating. He is completely in charge of his choir, and his leadership style contrasts with Ralph's.

Jack's hunting instinct is both self-destructive and lacking in foresight. Two example illustrate this: the boys killing the sow which could have bred and provided future meat; and, in their hunt for Ralph, the boys destroying the fruit trees. These two over-hasty actions mean that the boys would eventually have starved.

iggy

HO IS PIGGY?

gy is overweight, concerned about his health and doesn't
manual labour. Unlike Ralph, Jack and the choirboys, he
early working class. Piggy is arguably the most intelligent
on the island.

HAT DOES PIGGY DO IN THE NOVEL?

Piggy is the first boy to meet Ralph (see p. 1).

Piggy is the first to suggest he and Ralph have 'to do
something' (see p. 10).

Piggy suggests the conch is used to 'call the others' and 'Have a meeting' (see p. 12).

Piggy suggests the only fear on the island should be the fear 'of people' (see p. 90).

Piggy tells Ralph he will carry the conch to Castle Rock and confront Jack (see p. 189).

Piggy is killed by a giant rock released by Roger (see pp. 200–1).

OW IS PIGGY DESCRIBED AND WHAT DOES IT MEAN?

Quotation	Means?
e was shorter than the fair boy d very fat.'	Piggy's size sets him apart from the other boys and makes him different.
ggy was an outsider, not only accent, which did not matter, t by fat, and ass-mar, and ecs, and a certain disinclination r manual labour.'	Piggy appears to have little in his favour when survival on a desert island is at stake. He is an outsider immediately loathed and bullied by Jack.
em that haven't no common nse'	Piggy, for all his physical problems, is intelligent. Here, he is able to put his finger on the cause of the trouble among the boys.
e could find out how to make mall hot fire and then put een branches on to make oke.'	Piggy can solve problems using rational thought. He addresses the problem of making an easily tended fire with sufficient smoke to attract a ship.

EXAMINER'S TIP

When writing about **characters**, it is a good idea to show how others view them. How does Ralph view Piggy early on and later in the novel? How do the others generally view Piggy?

GRADE BOOSTER

Find three more quotes to show that Piggy is probably the most intelligent boy on the island. Try to choose quotes that show his organising ability and his practical advice.

XAMINER'S TIP: WRITING ABOUT PIGGY

is worth mentioning what Piggy represents. In a sense he represents the adult
ewpoint. He is brought up by his aunt and appears to have the foresight
d good sense of an older person. He exhibits a degree of caution and some
ganising ability. He **symbolises** attributes of civilisation in that he upholds the
premacy of the conch. He also has a strong sense of fair play and order. He
sses on to Ralph the ability to think clearly and logically.

Simon

WHO IS SIMON?

Simon enters the novel as one of Jack's choirboys. He faints and is often referred to as strange. He is the only boy who discovers the truth about the beast.

WHAT DOES SIMON DO IN THE NOVEL?

- Simon has a fainting fit as Jack leads his choir along the beach (see p. 16).
- Simon joins Ralph and Jack to explore parts of the island (see p. 20).
- Simon goes off alone into the jungle (see p. 56).
- Simon gives his piece of meat to Piggy (see p. 78).
- Simon 'communicates' with the 'Lord of the Flies' and loses consciousness (see p. 159).
- Simon discovers the dead parachutist and is killed when he comes to tell the bo the truth about the beast (see pp. 161, 168–169).

HOW IS SIMON DESCRIBED AND WHAT DOES IT MEAN?

Quotation	Means?
'batty', 'queer', 'funny', 'cracked'	Simon is prone to fainting fits and spends time alone. His 'strangeness' is never made explicit. The short quotes show the boys' lack of vocabulary to define him.
'What's the dirtiest thing there is?'	Simon is unable to explain the notion of evil, which manifests itself in the idea of 'the fear and 'the beast'. He has the intelligence and maturity to understand the concept, but lack the necessary language skills to express it.
'The beast was harmless and horrible.'	Simon understands the nature of the beast (the dead parachutist) and the significance of this for the boys ... that there is nothing to fear and there is life outside the island.
'In Simon's right temple, a pulse began to beat on the brain.'	Simon has considerable strength of mind but his body is frail. This shows his perceptiveness and individuality but also his vulnerability.

GRADE BOOSTER

Simon does not say much in the book. However, he can say words of great significance in a single sentence. For example, he tells Ralph that he will get back home. Find two other examples where Simon's words are very significant.

EXAMINER'S TIP

Reread the part in Chapter Nine where Simon is murdered. Whose viewpoint is given in this part of the novel? We certainly do not see events from Simon's perspective! Look for other viewpoints in other parts of the novel.

EXAMINER'S TIP: WRITING ABOUT SIMON

Simon is described by Jack as 'always about' (p. 56). He is loyal and is the only bo who helps Ralph with the third shelter. However, he does spend time alone.

Simon is often regarded as a prophet – even a saint or Christ-like figure. He is the one who confronts the 'Lord of the Flies', which symbolises Jack's evil. He is murdered bringing the truth back to the other boys. Had he lived to tell them th truth, he would have destroyed Jack's power over the other boys.

oger and Maurice

HO ARE ROGER AND MAURICE?

er is Jack's lieutenant. He has a sadistic streak. Maurice
oger's henchman.

HAT DO ROGER AND MAURICE DO IN
E NOVEL?

Roger and Maurice are part of Jack's choir (see p. 18).

Roger and Maurice destroy the littluns' sandcastles and
kick sand in Percival's eye (see p. 62).

Roger, concealed by a tree, teases a littlun by throwing
tones aimed to land close by (see pp. 64–5).

Roger is the first person Jack shows the mask clay to (see p. 65).

Roger acts 'with a sense of delirious abandonment' when he brings about Piggy's
death (see p. 200).

Roger has a stick sharpened 'at both ends' when the boys hunt Ralph (see p. 211).

OW ARE ROGER AND MAURICE DESCRIBED AND WHAT
ES IT MEAN?

Quotation	Means?
ou don't know Roger. He's a ror.'	Roger is the boy who most obviously turns from a choirboy into a pre-meditated killer. He outstrips Jack in barbarism.
aurice still felt the unease wrong-doing.'	When Roger and Maurice kick sand in Percival's eye, Maurice feels guilty. He retains a sense of sin.
oger advanced upon them one wielding a nameless thority.'	Roger is the person who administers torture. He appears to enjoy his role and will be backed up by Jack.
only Roger–'	Jack and Roger are described as 'terrors' here but the suggestion is that Roger will go further than Jack. Roger shows no remorse for the death of Piggy. He is willing to kill Ralph and place his head on a stick.

XAMINER'S TIP: WRITING ABOUT ROGER AND MAURICE

is easy to by-pass Roger's role in the novel. Without Roger, Piggy would have
ved. All the boys were involved in Simon's death, but did Roger deliberately kill
ggy or was the rock fall an accident?

ertainly, Roger showed no remorse for the death. He quickly went about his
usiness of forcing Sam and Eric to join Jack's tribe. Would any other character in
e book sharpen a stick 'at both ends' (p. 211)?

aurice remains much the same throughout the novel. He becomes a loyal
vage, as he was a loyal choirboy. He is solid and unimaginative.

GRADE BOOSTER

Avoid confusing the names and roles of some minor **characters**. Roger is Jack's number two and Maurice is Roger's number two. Robert is one of Jack's hunters. Flick through the novel and write notes about Robert's role.

EXAMINER'S TIP

Don't forget the littluns! Throughout the novel, they remain mostly anonymous. However, Golding deliberately gives the boy with the birthmark a distinguishing feature. The birthmark makes him memorable. After the over-zealous fire-lighting on the mountain, it is obvious that the boy is missing!

GRADE BOOSTER

The parachutist mistaken for the beast plays a crucial role. Having asked for a sign from the outside world, the dead airman is not what the boys had in mind. They do not see him for what he is – a dead human being – but rather as a representation of defeat, death and decay.

EXAMINER'S TIP

The move away from civilised behaviour towards tribalism happens early on. Notice how Percival Wemys Madison's conditioned response begins to dwindle. He fails to remember his phone number and later he 'sought in his head for an incantation that had faded clean away' (Chapter Twelve, p. 224). Minor characters are used to give clues as to what is happening in the novel.

Sam and Eric

WHO ARE SAM AND ERIC?

Sam and Eric are twins who do everything together. When they first appear, they are described as boys who 'breathed together' and 'grinned together' (p. 15).

WHAT DO SAM AND ERIC DO IN THE NOVEL?

- Sam and Eric look after the fire but they fall asleep and almost let it out (see p. 104).
- Sam and Eric believe the parachutist is the beast (see p. 107).
- Sam and Eric mention the beast's teeth and claws, its eyes and the way it 'kind sat up' (see p. 109).
- Sam and Eric stay with Ralph. They are loyal until they are forced to join Jack's tribe (see p. 198).
- Sam and Eric are to be tortured by Roger (see p. 202).
- Sam and Eric warn Ralph about Jack and Roger's intentions to harm him (see p. 2

HOW ARE SAM AND ERIC DESCRIBED AND WHAT DOES IT MEAN?

Quotation	Means?
'the twins shook their heads and pointed at each other and the crowd laughed.'	The twins are so alike that nobody can tell them apart. At first, this brings some humour into the novel.
'By custom now one conch did for both twins, for their substantial unity was recognized.'	When Sam and Eric tell of their encounter with the beast, it is as if they are telling the tale in stereo, which adds a frightening impact to the story.
'You lemme go—' '—and me.'	The twins are brave when confronted by Jack. They refuse to join the tribe and only give in when Roger forces them to. Even so, they do not wear tribal face paint.
'They're going to hunt you to-morrow.'	The twins warn Ralph that he will be hunted and killed, which suggests they would like to be on his side still. They retain civilised values but are made to do what Jack wants.

The naval officer and the parachutist

Check that you focus on the right thing when writing about the naval officer. Is it just that he arrives to rescue the boys and is dismayed when he discovers they have failed to 'put up a better show' (p. 224)? In one respect, he offers a sanitised view of the war. Dressed in his white, tropical kit, he could appear like a rescuing knight in shining armour. However, there is **irony** in the boys being returned to the same war that caused the death of the parachutist – a 'war' no less brutal than that whi afflicted the boys on the island. When writing about the parachutist, do mention what he represented for the boys.

rogress and revision check

EVISION ACTIVITY

How is Ralph described? (Write your answers below)

....

What does Ralph think about Jack at the beginning of the novel and how do his feelings change towards Jack?

....

Why does Jack paint his face? (Look for two reasons.)

....

Why is Jack's hunting instinct self-destructive?

....

Why is Piggy probably the most intelligent boy on the island?

....

EVISION ACTIVITY

n a piece of paper write down answers to these questions:

Choose a character whom you liked or disliked and follow their part in the novel.

Start: *A character I particularly liked (or disliked) was ... and the part he played in the novel was ...*

Look at the character of Simon. Is he an important character or not?

Start: *I believe Simon is (is not) an important character because ...*

GRADE BOOSTER

nswer this longer, practice question about the characters of the novel:

: Examine the characters of Ralph and Piggy. Explore their relationship as it hanges and develops through the novel. Think about ...

How Ralph views Piggy when they first meet

The way in which Piggy suggests ideas to Ralph

How Ralph's ideas towards Piggy change

The legacy Piggy leaves Ralph

or a C grade: check that you have mentioned all the relevant facts and use PEE point/evidence/explanation) when you quote from the text.

or an A grade: make sure you interpret the ideas behind the spoken words. Use your wn original ideas but back them up by using evidence from the text (PEE). Then evelop them by analysing in depth and detail particular key moments or dialogues.

Key contexts

THE AUTHOR

William Golding, the son of a school master, was born in Cornwall on 19 September 1911. He studied Natural Sciences and then English at Brasenose College, Oxford.

Later, Golding worked as an actor, producer and writer before teaching at Bishop Wordsworth's School, Salisbury. When the Second World War broke out, he served the Royal Navy.

Lord of the Flies was published in 1954 and in 1961 Golding became a full-time writer. His books sold well and he received the Nobel Prize for Literature in 1983. died on 19 June 1993.

 Personal experiences

Two important elements of Golding's life and experience are powerfully reflected *Lord of the Flies*:

- His pessimism after the Second World War (see also **Key themes: Cold War parano**
- His insight, drawn from his life as a school master, into children's behaviour.

Golding sets the story in an age when the adult world is at war and the children a evacuated from the war zone. The boys' descent into barbarism reflects Golding's belief that people are innately evil. He was appalled at what human beings can do one another. The children, as the novel closes, are prepared to kill each other.

EXAMINER'S TIP: WRITING ABOUT EVIL

Golding witnessed the war period and viewed this as a catalyst that released an already present evil – the original sinfulness of mankind. This trait he regarded as fundamental and permanent, able to emerge at any time and under any condition

Golding viewed children as potentially evil and sadistic. In this novel, we see stark examples of their cruelty. Jack mocks Piggy and is cruel to him from the firs chapter. When Piggy suggests he can help to explore the island, Jack declares 'W don't want you' (p. 21). Later on, Roger is cruel to the littluns and is willing to torture the twins.

BACKGROUND

Public school

It is no accident that Jack and his choir come from a particularly rigid school background. Choirboys are, by their nature, elitist. The boys would have been mos familiar with an organisational structure that was hierarchical, ordered and strict. the 1940s, beatings, by boys and by masters, would have been commonplace in stri schools. Given Jack's past conditioning, and the sudden absence of that strict regim it is perhaps not surprising that his deeper self is released in the way we witness.

ding's teaching experience at a public school allows him to portray Jack and choirboys realistically. Jack is clearly in charge of his choir, even after the public ool structure breaks down on the island. Roger, his henchman, would have been school bully.

the island, Roger appears to be allowed free reign to unleash his evil desires, le Jack is top of the hierarchy and the boys follow his strict commands, believing y cannot go against his orders. Jack's desire to be chief is based on the fact that s chapter chorister and head boy and he can 'sing C sharp' (Chapter One, p. 18), ich he feels gives him a higher status.

oys' behaviour

all the boys in the novel were from a public school culture. However, the boys in some common ways. To an extent their behaviour is reminiscent of the 1940s 1950s comic book heroes like 'Roy of the Rovers', and figures of fun like Frank ards's 'Billy Bunter' have clearly influenced the way in which Golding portrays boys.

y are initially fun-loving, with a boyish good humour. They also have a sense of ural decency. All of this changes as the novel progresses.

boys' language remains mild, however, even under extreme provocation. Jack s the most extreme language towards the end of the novel.

etting and place

need to be aware that the island is, in itself, a neutral place. The evil is within boys. However, Golding uses the elements and creatures to foreshadow what will ur later.

ph feels that the island is good but the weather when the boys arrive is bad and the urful bird gives a witch-like cry, which suggests that bad things will happen.

ore Simon's death, a storm is brewing and Golding writes, 'Evening was come, not h calm beauty but with the threat of violence' (Chapter Nine, p. 165). Here the nd is in harmony with the boys' feelings and actions.

the novel ends, the island's vegetation is consumed with fire as the boys attempt smoke out Ralph. Perhaps the island is the world in microcosm – a smaller version the whole. As the adults destroy their world, so the boys are destroying the island.

DID YOU KNOW

Golding's nickname as a teacher was 'Scruff'.

DID YOU KNOW

Rational and irrational thought are placed in context by Golding. Rational thought (as expressed at first by Piggy and later by Ralph) will lead to civilised behaviour, and irrational thought will ultimately lead to barbarism. The conch and the assembly meetings are products of rational thinking. The killing of the sow and the destruction of the fruit trees are a product of irrational behaviour.

KEY CONNECTIONS

Another famous island is featured in Shakespeare's play *The Tempest*. How does it compare with the island in *Lord of the Flies*?

Key themes

DID YOU KNOW

Golding once said 'man produces evil as a bee produces honey'. Can we detect Golding's statement in *Lord of the Flies*?

GOOD AND EVIL

The battle between good and evil is a central theme of *Lord of the Flies*. It appears in many conflicts – between the conch group and the savages; between the boys and the terrifying 'beast'; and between attempts at rescue from a passing ship and imprisonment on the increasingly chaotic island; to name but a few.

Early in the novel, good is in the ascendency. The conch provides a symbol of the decency and order of the society that the boys have come from. Ralph organises the construction of the shelters – mostly, in fact, the selfless work of himself and Simon – and a fire to signal to ships. The boys spend the majority of their time playing and there are few accidents – although one is serious: the fire that kills the boy with the birthmark. With Ralph's government, good is always a dominant force.

When Jack forms his own tribe, evil takes control. Only the naval officer's intervention prevents its complete triumph over good.

REVISION ACTIVITY

Here are some key moments for this theme. Are there any others?

- The conflict of good and evil is seen when Jack wants to hunt for meat but Ralph insists that shelters are built.

  'And we want shelters. Besides, the rest of your hunters came back hours ago. They've been swimming.' (p. 51)

- Roger's evil intentions are shown early on, when he wilfully destroys the littluns' game.

  'Roger led the way straight through the castles, kicking them over, burying the flowers, scattering the chosen stones.' (p. 62)

- Jack fails in his second bid to be leader. He refuses to stay with the conch group which is a small victory for good.

  'I'm going off by myself. He can catch his own pigs. Anyone who wants to hunt when I do can come too.' (p. 140)

- Jack's tribe are willing to take what they want. They steal Piggy's glasses to light their fire. Their attitude has become 'might is right'.

  'He was a chief now in truth; and he made stabbing motions with his spear. From his left hand dangled Piggy's broken glasses.' (p. 186)

EXAMINER'S TIP

When writing about good and evil, use examples from the novel. Find two more examples of good and evil, write down why the examples chosen are appropriate and find a relevant quote to back up your ideas.

RDER AND DISCIPLINE

ding was unhappy with the English public school tradition that insisted firm ipline was the best means of turning children into young adults.

re are no adults on the island. By removing them, the author sets free the impulses desires of the schoolboys and – almost – allows them to run their full course.

k first wrecks Ralph and Piggy's sensible plans, then becomes a dictator, and lly a murderer. Piggy, on the other hand, is a permanent victim of Jack's bullying d is killed. Clearly, these disasters could have been prevented by the normal lerliness of school.

olding despairing of the school system he taught in? Not necessarily, for Piggy's ins and Ralph's self-discipline result in positive achievements early in the novel, h as building a fire and shelters. School discipline might have restricted Jack's rst excesses. Difficulties only arise when the arbitrary discipline of a cruel leader – k – emerges.

at is needed is a balance between firm discipline and a certain creative freedom, d it is the absence of this that Golding is criticising in the schools of the time.

EVISION ACTIVITY

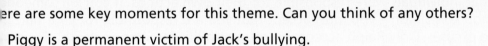

ere are some key moments for this theme. Can you think of any others?

Piggy is a permanent victim of Jack's bullying.

' "Here – Let me go!" His voice rose to a shriek of terror as Jack snatched the glasses off his face. "Mind out! Give 'em back! I can hardly see!" ' (p. 40)

Jack was, we presume, arrogant and bullying at school. He demonstrates these traits on the island.

' "You're talking too much," said Jack Merridew. "Shut up, Fatty." ' (p. 17)

Without discipline, the boys' worse excesses are revealed.

'Jack had him by the hair and was brandishing his knife.' (p. 125)

? DID YOU KNOW

Golding was a keen officer in the school's cadet corps. In 1943, to celebrate the honoured visit of the Russian colonel, the boys conducted fleet manoeuvres on the school field – mounted on bicycles.

EXAMINER'S TIP

Exploring the themes of *Lord of the Flies* throws light on what Golding wanted to say and the times he was writing in. In addition to the themes mentioned in these Notes, it is useful to think about others of your own.

? DID YOU KNOW

You can check the internet. A range of past and present front covers for the novel can be found online. Which do you think is the most effective and why?

CROWD MENTALITY

At the start of the novel, we find a natural group already formed when Jack appears at the head of the choir. The discipline within this group is of great help in hunting pigs, when good organisation is very important.

As order on the island breaks down, the boys begin to behave differently when in groups. Pig hunts become ritualised and frenzied, marked by chants such as, '*Kill the pig! Cut his throat! ... Bash him in!*' (Chapter Seven, p. 125). The boys act as a mob at these times and start to lose their individual identities. This (they feel) absolves them any direct blame for what happens and distracts them from their plight on the island.

The **climax** of this crowd mentality comes when Simon returns with the news that the beast is actually a dead pilot. He stumbles into the middle of the near-hysterical savages during a night-time thunderstorm, and is mistaken for the beast. The mob including Ralph, '*leapt on to the beast, screamed, struck, bit, tore. There were no words, and no movements but the tearing of teeth and claws*' (Chapter Nine, p. 16 The boys act like an extreme version of a crowd out of control at a football match a pop concert.

Individual responsibility

The issue of individual responsibility arises within the novel. It is important to be aware that Golding was influenced by **existentialism** and its **philosophers**. They claimed that individuals were responsible for their own actions. If you kill someone – as the mob kills Simon – you must accept that you are responsible for your part in it, with no excuses. Only Ralph accepts his responsibility for Simon's death: '*That w murder*' (Chapter Ten, p. 172). Look again at the excuses the other boys make for Simon's death.

REVISION ACTIVITY

Here are some key moments for this **theme**. Can you think of any others?

- Jack becomes a totalitarian leader.

  'Jack rose from the log that was his throne and sauntered to the edge of the grass.' (p. 165)

- The mob mentality is seen in the mob chant.

  '*Kill the beast! Cut his throat! Spill his blood!*' (p. 168)

- Individuality is lost during the tribal chant.

  'The movement became regular while the chant lost its first superficial excitement and began to beat like a steady pulse.' (p. 168)

- The mob is willing to kill.

  'There were no words, and no movements but the tearing of teeth and claws.' (p. 169)

OLD WAR PARANOIA

e first use of atomic weapons in war – at Hiroshima in Japan on 6 August 1945 – dermined many people's assumptions about life. Suddenly it seemed possible for whole of civilisation to be destroyed by a single conflict.

s was not a practical problem on a global scale until 1949, when the Soviet Union ploded its first A-bomb and the Cold War began in earnest. This was never an open r, although numerous conflicts were fought in its name. It became an ideological tle in which everyone suspected of being the enemy would be attacked.

ough the late 1940s and early 1950s many respected and influential people were troyed by (often false) accusations that they were communists. It was in this text that Golding wrote *Lord of the Flies*. A great deal of its stark confrontation – k against Ralph, savages against the conch group, even evil against good – stems m the Cold War outlook.

re specifically, the boys have been stranded by the Cold War turning into a real r. Their plane, presumably, has been shot down and the 'beast' is the pilot who has cted from his war plane.

EVISION ACTIVITY

ere are some key moments for this theme. Are there any others?

There is often stark confrontation between Ralph and Jack, which is reminiscent of Cold War rhetoric.

'You let the fire out.' (p. 73)

The boys are often unwilling to negotiate. When Simon tries to speak, he is brutally silenced. Notice the exclamation marks to indicate the words are commands.

'Sit down!'; 'Shut up!' (p. 96)

The boys ask for a sign from the outside world.

'If only they could send us something grown-up ... a sign or something.' (p. 102)

The sign sent by the grown-ups is a dead parachutist. The beast is a dead pilot showing that the adult world is at war.

'the figure sat on the mountain-top and bowed and sank and bowed again.' (p. 104)

TERNAL AND EXTERNAL CONFLICT

ere are two types of conflict in literature – external and internal. External conflict vhen a human is up against another human, an animal, the forces of nature or y other thing outside of himself. Internal conflict is when a person struggles with rces within himself.

DID YOU KNOW

The Cold War involved the USSR (now Russia) and the USA, powerful nations with nuclear weapons. Both sides were afraid of each other, so they avoided a direct conflict. They involved themselves in minor conflicts in different parts of the world. They threatened each other but avoided an all-out nuclear war.

GRADE BOOSTER

Examples in the novel of **external conflict** include: building the shelters against the forces of nature; the fear of the beast; the hatred between the boys; the hunting of pigs. Examples of **internal conflict** include: Simon struggling to articulate his thoughts; Ralph unable to stop the shutters coming down in his mind. Can you think of two more examples of external and internal conflict within the novel?

Progress and revision check

REVISION ACTIVITY

① What is happening in the outside world while the boys are stranded on the island? (Write your answers below)

....

② What does the death of the airman signify?

....

③ Why is the theme of good and evil central to this novel?

....

④ Why did Golding include discipline as a theme in the novel, and what evidence is there of a mob theme in *Lord of the Flies*?

....

⑤ Why do the boys, when in conflict, speak to each other using command sentences?

....

REVISION ACTIVITY

On a piece of paper write down answers to these questions:

● Would you consider 'Law and Order' to be a theme in the novel?

Start: *I would consider 'Law and Order' to be a theme in the novel because ...*

● Think about the theme of war and conflict. Where is this most obvious in the novel?

Start: *The theme of war and conflict is most obvious in the novel where ...*

GRADE BOOSTER

Answer this longer, practice question about the role of order in the novel:

Q: How is order initially established on the island? Think about ...

● The use of the conch to assemble the boys
● The use of a democratic vote
● Speaking at meetings
● The need for a fire to signal to ships – to aid the chances of rescue

For a C grade: you will need to show clear evidence of understanding key meanings in the text. Also, look for more significant or deeper interpretations.

For an A grade: you will need to demonstrate real engagement with the writer's ideas, selecting not just relevant quotations but also very carefully selected evidence, viewed in an original way.

Language

...are some useful terms to know when studying *Lord of the Flies*, what they ...an, and how they appear in the novel.

...terary term	Means?	Example
...legory	The depiction of a person close in character and behaviour to someone else in a different context.	Jack's power-hungry manner is often likened to that of Hitler.
...agery	The writer uses 'pictures' that reflect something else. The reader can imagine these pictures.	'Darkness poured out'
...ony	Seemingly good events lead to bad, and vice versa.	It is ironic that in attempting to rescue the boys from their own violent fears, Simon is himself killed.
...nomatopoeia	Some words sound like, and echo, the action they describe. In *Lord of the Flies* these words are used to convey the flight of a hurled stone and the sound of a spear.	'Zup' and 'Pht'
...mbolism	In this novel, symbolism is tied to objects.	The conch is more than just a shell. Like a church bell, it calls believers to a place of community, and symbolises democracy and fairness.

GRADE BOOSTER

When writing about **similes**, you will need to mention their effect. For example, Golding describes Ralph's hair as 'tapped like the tendrils of a creeper' (p. 203). With this simile the author creates a vivid picture of Ralph's matted, long hair.

DID YOU KNOW

Golding used to read the chapters of *Lord of the Flies* as he finished them to his Year 11 English class – and get them to do the proofreading for him!

...HE LANGUAGE CHARACTERS SPEAK

...e language spoken by the boys is very reminiscent of the 1950s and early 1960s. ...ost of the boys speak middle-class standard English, the exception being Piggy.

...gy's speech is obviously working class and punctuated by grammatical errors, such as ...idn't expect nothing' (Chapter One, p. 8). Notice the double negative. The other boys ...ght have said, 'I didn't expect anything.' It appears, though, that Piggy's speech and ...ss differences are not important to the boys. What makes Piggy different is his weight ...d the fact that he is a hypochondriac (he worries excessively about his health).

...ck is the one boy who uses inappropriate language. He is often rude ('You shut up, ...u fat slug!' (Chapter Five, p. 98). His aggressive language reflects his personality. ...lding has deliberately made both Piggy and Jack different, so that their **characters** ...nd out.

Colloquial speech

Notice the boys' use of colloquial speech. Although some speech indicates class differences, all the boys use ordinary speech as if they are in an ordinary situation. For example: 'You could get someone to dress up as a pig and then he could act— you know, pretend to knock me over and all that—' (Jack in Chapter Seven, p. 126) Do mention this, if appropriate, in your essays.

IRONY

Irony is the use of words to express something different from, and often opposite t their literal meaning. Examples of irony in *Lord of the Flies* are:

● The survivors of the plane crash are boys evacuated from a battle zone in a wor war. It is ironic that the society they form eventually breaks down and the boys are 'at war' with one another.

● Piggy has weak eyesight but his insight is strong.

● The naval officer who rescues the boys appears to be a knight in shining armou He represents civilisation and grown-up society. However, he also represents a world at war. His world is a mirror image, on a large scale, of the island – which the boys are destroying.

● Ralph is keen, throughout the novel, to keep a fire going – so that the boys can have a chance of being rescued. Jack is more interested in hunting. When Jack starts a fire to chase Ralph from his hiding place, his fire is seen by a passing ship Ironically, Jack aids the rescue!

SYMBOLISM

Symbolism in literature is the art of attributing symbolic meanings or significance t objects, events or titles.

The Lord of the Flies

● The title, *Lord of the Flies*, is symbolic. Beelzebub is the devil or Satan and he is often referred to as 'lord of the flies'.

● The evil, though, is not in the pig's head but within the boys themselves.

● The pig's head symbolises the evil in every man's heart. The pig's head attracts flies as it decays, a symbol of ruin and corruption, and becomes 'lord' of those same flies, which multiply, presumably.

Corruption

● The forest scar is a path of destruction through the forest (caused by the crashir plane) and can be seen as the encroachment of corrupt civilisation (or the boys) onto the island.

● The setting itself is a microcosm (smaller version) of the world, symbolising the corruptness of humanity.

KEY CONNECTIONS

The island itself can be seen as a metaphor for the Earth after a nuclear holocaust. Einstein once claimed that if the next world war was nuclear, the following war would be fought with bows and arrows.

arden of Eden

The island is a perfect place (the Garden of Eden) before the arrival of the boys. After the boys inhabit and partially destroy the island, it can be seen as the corrupted world of mankind.

vilised values

The death of Piggy and the destruction of the conch are symbolic of the failure to establish and retain civilised values in the world.

ope

The signal fire is a sign of hope. When it is allowed to go out, hope also dies.

ar and superstition

The beast can represent the boys' fear and superstitions. Jack plays on these fears to get his own way.

he dead parachutist

The dead parachutist symbolises the beast that the boys are so frightened of. In another way, the parachutist can be seen as the beast because he was taking part in a war to kill other human beings.

uthority

The log that Ralph sits on represents the symbol of authority. When Jack sits on a log as chief, it represents a throne.

riginal sin

Killing the first pig can represent original sin. As Adam and Eve ate the forbidden fruit in the biblical Garden of Eden, so the boys commit their first killing.

XAMINER'S TIP: WRITING ABOUT LANGUAGE

When you write about language, think about its impact on the reader. It is not nough to mention when (for example) onomatopoeia is used in the novel. You eed to mention the effect it has on events or on the reader.

or instance, when Ralph pretends to be a fighter plane and 'machine-gunned iggy', he uses the sound of a fighter plane: 'Sche-aa-ow!' (Chapter One, p. 6). lthough he is having fun, the world he has just left is involved in a violent war. oes this represent violent society and can it foreshadow the death of Piggy, when e is hit by the rock?

EXAMINER'S TIP

When writing about language, make sure you give practical examples from the text, then use a relevant quote and explain its significance.

Structure

Lord of the Flies contains twelve titled chapters. The island setting means events are largely a product of the characters' reactions and relationships as they engage with each other and their environment.

The novel's structure is dictated by the characters and setting. Apart from the naval officer and the dead parachutist, no one arrives on the island except the boys, and one leaves – with the exception of the three who die, departing in a spiritual sense.

The boys are placed in a vacuum; the story is moved along and restructured by the social chemistry as it evolves in that restricted setting. The parachutist injects an important element, and the beast, in whatever form – dead pilot, the 'fear', or Simon mistakenly killed in its place – provides another source of tension.

The human conflicts and fear of the beast increase as the story develops. This runs alongside the gradual degeneration of morals and morale towards an inevitable climax.

CLIMAX

The climax of a novel can be:

- The turning point at which the conflict begins to resolve itself for better or worse
- The final and most exciting event in a series of events

In the first definition, the turning point in *Lord of the Flies* is when Jack walks out of the assembly, having been rejected as leader for the second time, and quickly forms his own tribe.

In the second definition, the climax occurs when Ralph and Jack fight and Roger releases the rock, killing Piggy and destroying the conch. There is then a sudden fall away at the end when Ralph, running for his life, is saved by the intervention of the naval officer.

TIME AND PLACE

The novel's structure can be considered as distinct 'blocks' of action and development. The events take place over a period of several weeks – how many is not clear. The passage of time is suggested by one boy's loss of memory and observations about the length of the boys' hair. We also witness the disintegration of law and order and the boys' changing attitudes.

Place is important too. The first chapter is mainly set on the beach, where there is law and order, but the lighting of the fire and its burning out of control take place on the mountain. Simon's conversation with the pig's head occurs in the jungle, while the final tragedies occur at Castle Rock – Jack's domain.

rogress and revision check

EVISION ACTIVITY

- Why does Piggy's speech differ from the speech of the other boys? (Write your answers below)

....

- What is irony? Can you think of an example of irony in the novel?

....

- Why are Piggy's glasses thought to be symbolic? What do they represent?

....

- How does the island setting determine the structure of the novel?

....

- Comment on how particular events show the passage of time in the novel.

....

EVISION ACTIVITY

n a piece of paper write down answers to these questions:

Can you find two examples of the use of imagery in *Lord of the Flies*?

Start: *One example of imagery in the novel would be …*

Find examples of onomatopoeia in the novel and explain the effects it has on the events described.

Start: *An example of onomatopoeia in the novel is …*

GRADE BOOSTER

nswer this longer, practice question:

: What does the conch symbolise in the novel and how effective is it?

hink about:

Law and order

Free speech

Ralph's style of government

The breakdown of order

or a C grade: you will need to demonstrate that you understand some of the ey **themes** and some significant symbolic meanings. These ideas will need to be ncorporated into your answers.

or an A grade: you will need to demonstrate that you clearly understand a broad ange of the writer's ideas and how he worked these ideas into the novel using hemes and symbolism. These ideas will need to be incorporated into your answers.

PART SIX: GRADE BOOSTER

Understanding the question

Questions in exams or controlled conditions often need **'decoding'**. Decoding the question helps to ensure that your answer will be relevant and refers to what you have been asked.

 UNDERSTAND EXAM LANGUAGE

Get used to exam and essay style language by looking at specimen questions and the words they use. For example:

Exam speak!	Means?	Example
'What do you think?'	This is asking for your opinions, backed up with evidence from the text.	In my opinion, the conch represents civilised order and good leadership.
'The methods Golding uses'	How he shows us what we are meant to think about a character/idea.	Golding shows us how desperate Jack is to kill a pig when he describes Jack's concentration when hunting (Chapter 3).
'How does the writer portray ...'	How does the writer give us a mind's eye picture of a character or an event.	The writer tells us a lot about Simon by using other characters to talk about him.

 'BREAK DOWN' THE QUESTION

Pick out the **key words** or phrases. For example:

Question: Is Jack a good leader? How does Golding **portray Jack** at the **start** of the novel and at the **end** of the novel?

● **Portray** – how does Golding show us what Jack is like?

● **Start** – how does Jack behave as leader of the choir?

● **End** – what sort of a leader has Jack become?

What does this tell you?

Focus on: Jack's attitude towards Simon when Simon faints; the unenthusiastic vote from his choir when he and Ralph are first suggested as leader; how his priorities differ from Ralph's; his lack of discussion and willingness to give orders; his willingness to allow Roger to torture others.

 KNOW YOUR LITERARY LANGUAGE!

When studying texts you will come across words such as theme, symbol, imagery and metaphor. Some of these words could come up in the question you are asked. Make sure you know what they mean before you use them!

lanning your answer

vital that you plan your response to the controlled assessment task or possible
m question carefully, and that you then follow your plan, if you are to gain the
her grades.

 ## DO THE RESEARCH!

en revising for the exam, or planning your response to the controlled assessment
, collect evidence (for example, quotations) that will support what you have to
. For example, if preparing to answer a question on how Golding has explored the
me of good and evil, you might list ideas as follows:

Key point	Evidence/quotation	Page/chapter, etc.
e conch provides a symbol of e decency and order of society. hen the conch is broken, evil s a free reign on the island.	'the conch exploded into a thousand white fragments'	Chapter Eleven, page 200

 ## PLAN FOR PARAGRAPHS

paragraphs to plan your answer. For example:

The first paragraph should **introduce** the **argument** you wish to make.

Then, jot down how the paragraphs that follow will **develop** this argument.
Include **details**, examples and other possible **points of view**. Each paragraph is
likely to deal with one point at a time.

Sum up your argument in the last paragraph.

example, for the following task:

estion: How does Golding present the character of Jack? Comment on the
language devices and techniques used.

imple plan:

Paragraph 1: *Introduction*

Paragraph 2: *First point*, e.g. **How Jack deals with Simon when Simon faints.**

Paragraph 3: *Second point*, e.g. **Jack's obsession with hunting pigs**.

Paragraph 4: *Third point*, e.g. **Jack's disagreements with Ralph and his second attempt at becoming leader.**

Paragraph 5: *Fourth point*, e.g. **Jack's leadership and his use of language**.

Paragraph 6: *Conclusion*

How to use quotations

One of the secrets of success in writing essays is to use quotations **effectively**. Ther are five basic principles:

❶ Put quotation marks, e.g. ' ', around the quotation.

❷ Write the quotation exactly as it appears in the original.

❸ Do not use a quotation that repeats what you have just written.

❹ Use the quotation so that it fits into your sentence, or, if it is longer, indent it as a separate paragraph.

❺ Only quote what is most useful.

TOP TIP USE QUOTATIONS TO DEVELOP YOUR ARGUMENT

Quotations should be used to develop the line of thought in your essays. Your comment should not duplicate what is in your quotation. For example:

GRADE D	GRADE C
(simply repeats the idea)	**(makes a point and supports it with a relevant quotation)**
Eric tells Ralph the boys are going to get him; 'They're going to do you' (Chapter Twelve, p. 209).	Golding shows that the tribe will hunt and kill Ralph when Eric says, 'They're going to do you' (Chapter Twelve, p. 209).

However, the most sophisticated way of using the writer's words is to embed them into your sentence, and further develop the point:

GRADE A

(makes point, embeds quote and develops idea)

Golding shows that the tribe have descended into savagery when Ralph is told by Eric 'They're going to do you' (Chapter Twelve, p. 209). The vague use of 'do' by Eric, which implies murder, shows that he still cannot bring himself to face the reality of the savagery and is still using the language of the playground.

When you use quotations in this way, you are demonstrating the ability to use text as evidence to support your ideas – not simply including words from the original to prove you have read it.

EXAMINER'S TIP

Try using a quotation to begin your response. You can use it as a launch-pad for your ideas, or as an idea you are going to argue against.

itting the examination

mination papers are carefully designed to give you the opportunity to do your
t. Follow these handy hints for exam success:

 ## BEFORE YOU START

Make sure that you **know the texts** you are writing about so that you are
properly prepared and equipped.

You need to be **comfortable** and **free from distractions**. Inform the invigilator
if anything is off-putting, e.g. a shaky desk.

Read and follow the instructions, or rubric, on the front of the examination
paper. You should know by now what you need to do but **check** to reassure
yourself.

Before beginning your answer have a **skim** through the **whole paper** to make
sure you don't miss anything **important**.

Observe the **time allocation** – and follow it carefully. If they recommend 45
minutes for a particular question on a text make sure this is how long you spend.

 ## WRITING YOUR RESPONSES

★ **GRADE BOOSTER**

Where
appropriate
refer to the
language
technique used
by the writer
and the effect
it creates. For
example, if
you say, 'this
metaphor shows
how ...', or 'the
effect of this
metaphor is
to emphasise
to the reader
...' this could
get you higher
marks.

 typical 45 minute examination essay is probably between 550 and 800 words
 length.

deally, spend a minimum of 5 minutes planning your answer before you begin.

se the questions to structure your response. Here is an example:

uestion: Do you see the ending of the novel as negative or positive? What
methods does the writer use to lead you to this view?

The introduction to your answer could briefly describe **the ending** of the novel;

the second part could explain what could be seen as **positive**;

the third part could be an exploration of the **negative** aspects;

the conclusion would **sum up your own viewpoint**.

or each part allocate paragraphs to cover the points you wish to make (see
lanning your answer).

eep your writing clear and easy to read, using paragraphs, and link words to
how the structure of your answers.

pend a couple of minutes afterwards quickly checking for obvious errors.

 ## 'KEY WORDS' ARE THE KEY!

ep on mentioning the **key words** from the question in your answer. This will keep
u on track and remind the examiner that you are answering the question set.

Sitting the controlled assessment

It may be the case that you are responding to *Lord of the Flies* in a controlled assessment situation. Follow these useful tips for success.

 ## WHAT YOU ARE REQUIRED TO DO

Make sure you are clear about:

- The **specific text** and **task** you are preparing (is it just *Lord of the Flies*, or mor[e] than one?)
- How **long** you have during the assessment period (i.e. 3–4 hours?)
- How **much** you are expected or allowed to write (i.e. 1,200 words?)
- **What** you are **allowed to take** into the controlled assessment, and what you can use (or not, as the case may be!). You may be able to take in brief notes BUT NOT draft answers, so check with your teacher.

 ## HOW YOU CAN PREPARE

Once you know your task, topic and text/s you can:

- Make **notes** and **prepare** the **points**, **evidence**, **quotations**, etc. you are likely to use.
- Practise or draft **model answers**.
- Use these **York Notes** to hone your **skills**, e.g. use of quotations, how to plan an answer and focus on what makes a **top grade**.

 ## DURING THE CONTROLLED ASSESSMENT

Remember:

- **Stick** to the topic and task you have been given.
- The allocated **time** is for **writing**, so make the most of it. It is double the time you might have in an exam, so you will be writing almost **twice as much** (or more).
- **If** you are **allowed** access to a **dictionary or thesaurus** make use of them; if no[t] don't go near them!
- At the end of the controlled assessment follow your **teacher's instructions**. Fo[r] example, make sure you have written your **name** clearly on all the pages you hand in.

GRADE BOOSTER

When talking about linguistic devices and figurative language, it is most important to describe the *effect* they have.

mprove your grade

 useful to know the type of responses examiners are looking for when they award
 erent grades. The following broad guidance should help you to improve your
 de when responding to the task you are set!

GRADE C

What you need to show	What this means
ustained **response** to task and text	You write enough! You don't run out of ideas after two paragraphs.
fective use of **details** to **support** ur explanations	You generally support what you say with evidence, e.g. When Piggy tells Ralph to 'call the others' we know he has ideas but is aware that he is not a leader.
xplanation of the writer's **use of** nguage, **structure**, **form**, etc., and e **effect on readers**	You must write about the writer's use of these things. It's not enough simply to give a viewpoint. So, you might comment on the boys' middle-class speech and find an appropriate quote.
ppropriate comment on **characters**, ot, **themes**, **ideas** and **settings**	What you say is relevant. If the task asks you to comment on how the theme of 'Law and Order' is developed, you will need to show this through the characters and their actions, using relevant quotes.

GRADE A

What you need to show *in addition* to the above	What this means
sightful, **exploratory** response to e text	You look beyond the obvious, going deeper into the novel, looking at the ideas behind the reason for writing the novel. You might question the idea of why Golding set the novel on an uninhabited island.
lose analysis and use of detail	If you are looking at the writer's use of language, you comment on each word in a sentence, drawing out its distinctive effect on the reader, e.g. ' "I ought to be chief," said Jack with simple arrogance.' How does each word build up a picture of Jack at this early stage of the novel?
onvincing and **imaginative** terpretation	Your viewpoint is likely to convince the examiner. You show you have *engaged* with the text, and come up with your own ideas. These may be based on what you have discussed in class or read about, but you have made your own decisions.

Annotated sample answers

This section will provide you with **two model answers**, one at **C grade** and one at **A grade**, to give you an idea of what is required to **achieve** at different levels.

> **Question:** Is Simon an important character or not? Write about:
>
> A His contribution to the novel
>
> B The methods Golding uses to show what Simon is like

CANDIDATE 1

Good use of quotation.

Simon is an important character as he makes some key contributions to the novel. He is first seen when he 'flopped on the sand'. He is physically weak but quite clever. Jack has no sympathy for Simon when he faints. 'He's always throwing a faint'. This tells us something about Jack's character.

Gives others opinions of the character.

Quotation not embedded into the sentence.

Correctly backs up statement.

Although most of the boys believe Simon is strange, he is also kind to the younger boys and he helps build the shelters, which proves he has a sense of responsibility. Simon is the only choirboy under Jack's charge who stays loyal to Ralph – the elected leader. Unlike the other choirboys, he doesn't become a hunter or, later on, a savage.

Not specific enou The point needs be expanded.

Correctly focuses on the passage.

Another point showing Simon is very important is that he is the only boy who understands what the beast is – a dead airman. Early on in the novel, Simon is mistaken for the beast as he wanders alone in the forest. Does this foreshadow his death? 'Simon's dead body moved out towards the open sea.'

Quote does not match the point made.

Need to provide example of the language used

Golding's methods of presenting Simon are to give us a physical description and show us his physical weaknesses. Some boys think he is strange ... wandering off alone and fainting. Through the language used, he appears gentle – telling Ralph that he will get home again.

The reader is shown that Simon is often able to think things through but he lacks the language skills and confidence to explain to others what he's actually thinking. Jack tells him to 'shut up' when he does try to make contributions to the discussions. 'Maybe,' he said hesitantly, 'Maybe there is a beast.'

Good understand of the text.

Unfortunately, Simon was never able to say what he really thought. He was unable to tell the savages the truth because he was killed.

Overall comment:

This is a solid essay with some clear points in each paragraph. Views are supported with some well-chosen quotations, however occasionally the points are not supported by evidence. There is some evidence of personal response, but greater reference to the language used to describe Simon's appearance and behaviour is needed.

GRADE C

NDIDATE 2

ell-chosen quote
n an explanation.

Golding first presents Simon as weak and of little value. Jack has no patience with him and Ralph suggests they 'talk over his head'. The reader may also feel little sympathy for him at this point. However, Simon provides an unusual perspective. When he describes the bushes poetically as 'like candles', 'with 'candle buds', this figurative language separates him from Jack, who dismisses Simon's radically different viewpoint of the bushes because they 'can't eat them'.

Original thought – to describe the way Simon sees things.

Good to point out events from another character's viewpoint.

Simon is important as the one member of Jack's choir who supports Ralph. Ralph learns to value his advice and loyalty. He has Simon in mind when he wants to explain 'how people were never quite what you thought they were.' He is, at this point, surprised at Simon's tenacity when building shelters. As readers perhaps we are changing our view of Simon, too.

Use of mature vocabulary.

Correctly moves on to the second part of the question.

inal ideas.

Golding uses various other methods to show what Simon is like. We learn that he is a 'skinny vivid little boy' with 'black and coarse hair', a description in direct contrast to Ralph's other confidant, Piggy. He is a quiet, complex character, who is kind and helpful as well as brave and mature. He spends time alone, being mistaken for the beast by the littluns – a foreshadowing of later events. He is unable to voice his thoughts, which suggests Golding wanted the reader to see his frailties, too. He was, in fact, a clever boy growing up!

Shows knowledge of linguistic techniques.

uote is needed
ack up some
inal ideas.

Simon's main contribution is his willingness to bring the truth to the others. Golding perhaps sees him as a symbol – a gentle Christ-like figure killed trying to tell the truth about the beast.

In conclusion, Simon is important because he has the intelligence and vision to see things as they actually are, his problem being that he is unable to express his thoughts clearly.

verall comment:

excellent response with few weak points. The main areas are discussed
lly. Quotations and evidence are woven skilfully into the answer, with several
ferences to Golding's use of language. The student demonstrates some original
inking and ideas. The second half is slightly weaker with, perhaps, not enough
scussion on Golding's methods.

GRADE A

Further questions

1 How do you respond to the first two chapters of *Lord of the Flies*?

Write about:
- What happens at the start of the novel and your response to these events
- How Golding uses details here that are important in the novel as a whole

2 How does Golding present Piggy in the novel?

Write about:
- What he does and what happens to him
- The methods Golding uses to present him

3 How does Golding present the relationship between Ralph and Jack?

Write about:
- Their feelings for each other and the way those feelings change as the novel progresses
- The methods Golding uses to present their relationship

4 Near the start of *Lord of the Flies* Ralph calls the island a good one. Is he right?

Write about:
- The events that happen on the island that might make Ralph change his mind
- The use of language and imagery in the novel

5 Examine the idea of good and evil in *Lord of the Flies*.

Write about:
- The effects of the events that happen on the island
- The way Golding presents good and evil

6 Choose a character from *Lord of the Flies*. Write an analysis of how he has been characterised through his actions, speech and opinions.

Write about:
- How an impression of that character has been created
- What others think and say about that character

7 Explore the theme of friendship and responsibility in the novel.

Write about:
- How the theme is developed in the early part of the novel
- The use of language to develop the theme

8 How has Golding created a voice that is both distinctive and individual in *Lord of the Flies*?

Write about:
- The ideas, language and themes of the novel
- The reasons why Golding wrote the novel

9 Compare Jack's descent into evil with Macbeth's descent into evil in Shakespeare's play.

Write about:
- How they differ and how they are similar
- Whether Golding and Shakespeare use any similar techniques to portray evil.

10 Discuss the use of imagery in *Lord of the Flies*.

Write about:
- Specific imagery and how each instance contributes to the novel
- The way in which Golding presents imagery in the novel

LITERARY TERMS

Literary term	Explanation
allegory	a story with two different meanings, where the straightforward meaning on the surface is used to reveal a deeper meaning underneath
atmosphere	a mood or feeling
character(s)	either a person in a play, novel, etc., or his or her personality
climax	the turning point at which the conflict begins to resolve itself or the final and most exciting event
colloquial	the everyday speech used by people in ordinary situations
dramatic irony	when the reader (audience) knows more about what is happening than some of the characters
flashback	a sudden jumping back to an earlier point in the narrative
foreshadow	act as a warning or sign of something that will occur later
imagery	descriptive language which uses images to make actions, objects and characters more vivid in the reader's mind. Metaphors and similes are examples of imagery
irony	when somebody deliberately says one thing when they mean another, usually in a humorous or sarcastic way
metaphor	when one thing is used to describe another thing to create a striking or unusual image
onomatopoeia	the use of words which sound like the noise they describe
pathetic fallacy	when the natural world, especially the weather, is used to reflect the feelings of characters
simile	when one thing is compared directly to another thing, using the words 'like' or 'as'
structure	the organisation or overall design of a work
symbolism	when an object, a person or a thing is used to represent another thing
theme	a central idea examined by an author

CHECKPOINT ANSWERS

CHECKPOINT 1

Two: Jack Merridew and Percy Wemys Madison.

CHECKPOINT 2

Possibly, as both want such different things. Ralph is concerned about surviving until they can be rescued; Jack just wants to enjoy himself.

CHECKPOINT 3

Students need to read the evidence on pages 51–2 with care.

CHECKPOINT 4

They are playing on the beach and swimming.

CHECKPOINT 5

Maurice.

CHECKPOINT 6

He enjoys the thrill of hunting.

CHECKPOINT 7

Their general dirtiness and lack of hygiene.

CHECKPOINT 8

He has been bullied in the past.

CHECKPOINT 9

His arrival on the island proves there is life outside. War has not annihilated (totally destroyed) civilisation.

CHECKPOINT 10

It enables him to understand the actions of others and how to have sympathy with them.

CHECKPOINT 11

They are arguing about courage ... or lack of it!

CHECKPOINT 12

He is relieved to see Jack gone.

CHECKPOINT 13

The voice of authority – the voice of one who is always right.

CHECKPOINT 14

Answers will vary.

CHECKPOINT 15

He is concerned about the other boys, particularly the safety of the younger children.

CHECKPOINT 16

They are both washed out to sea.

CHECKPOINT 17

He refers to it as an accident.

CHECKPOINT 18

He avoids discussions and issues orders.

CHECKPOINT 19

The conch.

CHECKPOINT 20

The savagery of the island.